BURIED IN THE SAND

A BIZZY DEVLIN COZY MYSTERY

TJ COSTELLO

PULLEN POINTE PUBLISHING

For all the angels in my life who kept whispering, or shouting, you can do it.

And to my pup, St. Peter "Petey" –thanks for stealing this girl's heart.

ACKNOWLEDGMENTS

So many people helped with this book, in big and small ways, and all of those contributions made this book happen.

My parents top the list because they brought me into the world, raised me, and paid for my college education. Thank you!

My sister and brothers have helped in so many ways with their support – Sissy, John, and Lee, thanks for believing in me.

Thank you, Kristelle, for reminding me how much I loved mysteries, and why I started to write in the first place.

To my editor, Anne Brewer, you really helped me hone this novel with your enthusiasm for cozies and story direction. Kim, thank you for the great covers. And to all my proofreaders, thank you for being so good with the details.

My 1667 group, you are my rock. Seriously. I have learned so much from each of you – yup, you all get a shout out: Anne, Lucinda, Lynda, Elise, Shari, Martina, Heather, and everyone else who has popped in since we began. You all are the bright and shining silver lining to a dark year.

Karen, the head cheerleader of 1667 and my coach,

you've been my touchstone. You've coached me not just with writing and publishing but with life and held me accountable with the details. I am so grateful.

To my writing group -Dianne, Lisa, Sherry, Shari, Martina, Karen, Anne-being with you guys is like being in a master class for writing every single session. This screenwriter and playwright turned into a full-fledged novelist with your guidance, and I credit our sessions for that. Thank you!

To the members of my other writing group, you helped me become a better writer through the years. Henry, Linda, Janet, Tim, and Kerry - thank you.

Maura, your friendship has been invaluable, and your fashion expertise has assured that I never leave the house dressed like a two-year old boy who picked out his own clothes.

Thank you Shéa, for reading long passages, making suggestions, editing when I asked, and letting me read it to you. Over and over. Thank you for being a pillar of support for a really long time. LALALA.

CHAPTER ONE

The orange rubber ball bobbed up and down in the small waves just after dawn. It didn't move too far out, but was still out of reach for Bizzy Devlin and her puppy, Luigi. Bizzy watched the ball, and Luigi barked - a loud, piercing bark. He'd take one step forward, and when the wave came toward him, he'd back away. The whole time he kept his eye on the ball.

"Go get it, Luigi!"

Bizzy gently nudged him toward the water. But every time the wave came near, the pup jumped back and then continued barking. He looked up at Bizzy.

"You do not seriously expect me to go into that icy water, do you?" It was New England ocean water in September. Warmer than May or June water, but certainly not Florida bath-temperature water.

"Come on Luigi, go get it. Run in, grab it with your mouth, and run out." She demonstrated for her dog, opening her mouth wide and pretending to grab the ball. She went to the water's edge, and when the water came back and almost hit her sneakers, she backed away, in unison with her apricot red Labradoodle. Still a pup, and a very curious pup, he was not willing to go into the cold water.

"It's your last ball. We won't be able to play ball until I get you some new ones." In reply, he looked at Bizzy and tilted his head both to the right and to the left, clearly indicating he was listening.

He turned back to the ball and barked even louder at the bobbing orange object not that far into the water.

Luigi stopped barking and began to whine. To Bizzy, he sounded like he was in pain. He nuzzled up beside her and licked her hand. "Oh, you think kisses will get you your ball?" She smiled and reached down to Luigi. He licked her hand again.

She sighed, reached down to untie her sneakers, and took them off. This part of the beach had gravel and rocks. Bizzy entered the ocean with her white athletic socks, hoping they would cushion the pain of stepping on the sharp gravel. "Oh boy, oh boy, this is cold!"

She turned back to the dog, who walked to the water's edge and then retreated with the next wave. Luigi focused his barking at her. Like any good dog-mother, Bizzy loved trying to figure out what her dog was thinking. She was convinced that Luigi loved Italian food as much as she did, and that he thought great thoughts as a human would.

Bizzy's photography assistant, Jacko, came up with Luigi's name. It was officially "Saint Luigi," but Bizzy dropped the "Saint" part of his name, especially when he did naughty things. "You're thinking, 'I got my human to go into the cold ocean to get my ball,'" she said out loud. She didn't turn back to see her dog's reaction. "You're also thinking, 'I have the best mommy ever.'"

At this she laughed. Then she slipped a little, nearly falling into the ocean that now covered her knees. The water nipped at her black lycra sports shorts and the old grey t-shirt that hung loosely over them, which, in turn, had a ripped old hoodie sweatshirt over that. Bizzy considered this her New England walk-on-the-beach fashion. Every time she got close to the ball, a wave picked it up and carried it just out of reach. Bizzy grit her teeth and reached as far as she could to swoop up the ball. At the same time, she lost her footing on the rocks and fell completely into the ocean. She screamed a little from the cold. As she stood up, the orange ball was now in the firm grasp of her right hand. "I got it, Luigi!" He yelped and barked and whined all at once. Bizzy trudged toward the beach, soaked from the ocean, a little piece of seaweed now stuck to her matted reddish brown hair. She removed the seaweed from her head as she reached the shore.

Bizzy picked up her sneakers, the only dry thing left, and started to walk back up the beach, her socks squishing with each step in the sand. Luigi lunged for the ball. "Oh no, little boy. I will *not* be giving you the ball at this time." She put the ball in her dripping hoodie pocket and continued to walk in her socks, now caked in sand, up the beach to a metal ramp that led to the seawall. Luigi followed her, or rather he followed the *ball*, nipping at her shorts.

"Don't you dare put a rip in these shorts, Lou. Don't you dare."

As Bizzy and Luigi walked up the beach toward the seawall, Lobsterman came walking past them toward the ocean with a bucket of fish heads, the bait for his lobster traps. He was one of the personalities of the Pointe seaside neighborhood. You could see him most days rowing out to his traps to bait them or bring in his catch of lobsters. He pretty much kept to himself and was a man of few words. "Good morning, Lobsterman," Bizzy said. She had heard his real name years before. But everyone just called him "Lobsterman," which is how he wanted it.

He nodded to her. "Bizzy," was his simple reply.

And that was as much as you were likely to hear from him.

On the other side of the seawall, Bizzy and Luigi walked down a few stairs toward a short row of seaside cottages crowded together. She tiptoed past her next door neighbor Edith's cottage to her own. The small houses were only a few feet apart.

The times Bizzy flew into Logan Airport, which passed over the little peninsula she lived on, the cluster of houses looked almost like a tightly woven tapestry. Those with a view from the air might think the people who lived in this little piece of congested land were crazy. *Yup, we are.* She imagined the pilgrims after just disembarking their ships saying, "It's been a long trip. This will do just fine." Bizzy laughed at the imagined conversations she'd come up with. "I'm not going one step further. I'm done," she heard her imagined travel-weary pilgrim woman say.

They left their ships and built little seaside cottages, and *did* stay. The absence of zoning laws meant people just built anywhere. They didn't realize their descendants would be fighting over every inch of land three centuries later.

That's not how it really happened, but Bizzy enjoyed the imaginary scenes she created. In reality, the land had been used as a seaside resort for the well-heeled of Boston in the 19th century, who would take the train or ferry to the little stretch of land jutting out into the ocean - near enough to Boston so that no one had to travel far, but still away from the congested city life. With the invention of the car, the privileged city people arrived to Pullen Pointe, known as

"The Pointe," to have their little piece of heaven. Others, though, drove down the dreaded expressway to Cape Cod. *Who wanted to spend four hours in traffic when you have this?* Bizzy thought when she viewed the sunrise every morning.

Everything in the small town, but especially the little sliver of land that protruded into the ocean, had revolutionary war history. And "The Pointe" apparently had been the site of a Paul Revere Smelting Factory. At least that was the agreed-upon rumor. Every so often some kid would pick up an old piece of metal, and someone would say, "Hey, that came from Paul Revere's factory."

Did it? Could Paul Revere even produce that much smelted metal? Well, it served as a history lesson.

Bizzy arrived home and opened her wooden gate, letting the dog enter first. The gate closed behind her with a bit of a bang. She winced and then stared at Luigi. "We'd better not have woken up Edy," she whispered to the dog.

He went behind the house to the hose. "How funny that you like the hose with water," she said softly to Luigi, "especially since you wouldn't go into the ocean to get your ball." What he really liked was to try and drink the water as she hosed him off. First she squirted his sandy paws. Luigi turned around and put his mouth over the spray coming from the hose. Usually that drenched her. Today it didn't matter. She hosed herself off, including her hair.

She picked up a towel that she had left outside before their walk. Now the games really began. Luigi jumped at the towel as she tried to dry him off, barking and giving Bizzy his play growl.

"Stop," she whispered. "You'll wake up Edy." Edy was Bizzy's best friend, and was an unofficial aunt to Luigi.

"It's okay LuLu. Edy's up," came a raspy, barely awake

voice from next door. "Ask your mommy if she wants a cup of very strong coffee."

Luigi ran over to Edy's door just as she opened it. Edy had the queen vibe going. She wore a purple satin scarf that covered most of her hair. A single long curl of black hair slipped out of the side, dangling along her dark brown cheek. *How do you look this good in the morning?* Bizzy wrung out her sopping wet t-shirt and hoodie.

"Love one," Bizzy said. "I just have to get some dry clothes on. I fell in the ocean."

Edy scanned her up and down and shook her head. "I think it's the dog who's supposed to fetch the ball."

Bizzy glared at Luigi. "Tell that to *him*." She headed for her front door, dripping wet.

"You'll have to bring your own creamer and sugar. You know I don't like anything interfering with the bitter taste of my black coffee."

Bizzy knew this was a friendly dig at the way she loved her coffee: more sugar and creamer than actual coffee.

Bizzy went into her house, leaving Luigi outside.

"Baby boy, come here so I can give you a treat," Bizzy heard Edy say.

A few minutes later, Bizzy came out of her house wearing jeans, a long sleeve t-shirt, and a long sweater. Her hair was now slung in a towel, twisted up like a turban. She had a carton of half-and-half, a sugar container, and a spoon hanging out of her mouth. Edy came out of the house with two coffee cups, steaming hot. She placed the coffees on a picnic table situated between their two houses. They had agreed to share the space between the two houses long ago and never thought about it again. The two women kept it quaint and beachy, more to Edy's credit than to Bizzy's.

Right now brightly colored mums lined both sides of the

old wooden deck. Down further, close to Edy's house, some hostas grew out of control. Edy would try to cut them back, but they'd soon come roaring back. Lately, Luigi loved to play in them. He'd dive in like a kamikaze pilot and dig and dig, until there were big holes in the hosta patch. Then he'd do it again.

"Oh Edy, there he goes again." Bizzy got up from her seat and turned toward her dog, saying, "Luigi, stop."

"Biz, I've been trying to kill those things forever. That baby boy is my secret weapon." Luigi ran up to Edy with hostas sticking out from his mouth and sticking to his body.

"Then why not get rid of them?"

Edy sighed, "A gift."

"Personally, I hate them. I think they're the lazy gardener's way of just having green around."

"Says the woman who puts four pots of red geraniums out every year and calls it a day. And," she paused as she pulled her cup up, "I take care of them."

"At least I don't kill them."

"No, Bizzy, because the entire neighborhood feels sorry for them and waters them."

"It kind of takes a village, huh?"

Both women laughed.

"Holy moly, lady, are you really going to put all that sugar in there?" Edy asked as she watched Bizzy spoon three heaping sugars into her coffee.

"How do you expect me to drink my coffee on *the veranda?*"

Edy took a big swallow. "It is perfectly wonderful."

"Wasn't that hot?" Bizzy looked at her friend in horror.

"Nah, I put in a few ice cubes to cool it down."

"Yuck," said Bizzy. "Not only do you like it black and strong, but you like it lukewarm to boot?"

"Yup," laughed Edy again. "I like it best when the pot has been sitting there a few hours, and it seems to be thickening on the bottom - "

"Oh, please stop. Please!" Bizzy put another teaspoon of sugar in her coffee.

"You realize it is barely 6:30 a.m., right?"

Bizzy nodded.

"And today's the day?" Edy leaned in a little. "Right?"

Bizzy nodded again.

"Yeah, it's time," Edy said.

Bizzy stared down into her coffee, swishing it around with the spoon and humming an old Carly Simon tune while focusing on the reflection of clouds in her coffee.

"Bizzy. It's time."

Bizzy took in a big breath. She removed the spoon from her coffee and licked the back of it. "I told Jacko I'd be in around 9 or 10."

"Oh, *that's* specific. Be there at 9 sharp. Work will be good for you."

"I don't really want to start again."

Luigi snuggled up to Bizzy. Edy smiled. "It seems you have, just by getting this little guy."

She leaned down to pet him, and then looked up to Edy. "I don't know if I could have gotten through this without you...and Jacko."

Edy took a big swig of her lukewarm black coffee and gave her the "Edy stare." It meant "do what I say," and Bizzy knew it.

"Yes ma'am!" Bizzy saluted. "I will be at work by 9 a.m. sharp."

CHAPTER TWO

Bizzy and Luigi jaunted down the boardwalk toward the street. Once at the street, Luigi came to a halt. Bizzy turned to him. "Yes, you are going in the car." He refused to move, so she pulled him toward the car. His paws slid across the sidewalk. The little guy, in the space of an instant, became a cement statue. His reaction to the car was the same now as when he went to the vet's office, and more recently, to the groomer's: perfectly uncooperative. *A cement furball.*

Bizzy managed to get Luigi near the car, and in one swoop, she picked him up, opened the door, and plopped him on the back seat. In the time it took her to get around to the driver's side, Luigi jumped to the front and sat in the driver's seat. She nudged him over to the passenger seat. He moved back over and sat on Bizzy's lap. "I'm going to get you your own car seat, buddy."

Bizzy took a deep breath. She was finally ready to get back to business. She loved her little blue Honda CR-V, but she didn't want to turn the key. *Just turn the key.*

Her assistant, Giacomo "Jacko" Rossi, had taken on the

bulk of the business efforts in her photography studio over the last several months. When Dan, her husband, died in a car accident seven months earlier, Bizzy couldn't function. Some days she barely managed to eat, let alone pick up a camera. Jacko, her nickname for her assistant, took care of everything in the studio.

She had done a first photo shoot with Jacko on location, but this was her first time back in the studio. Jacko had insisted she needed to start shooting in the studio again. People wanted *her*.

"Totally not true, Jacko," she said.

"Bizzy, just last week I couldn't get the bank manager to smile at his portrait session, because she specifically wanted *you*," he said.

She knew she had to get back to doing photography or lose the business. She kept thinking one day she'd wake up and everything would be okay. Her heart wouldn't hurt. And Dan would be there. At the time Dan died, the studio had been going gangbusters, and Bizzy barely got to see Dan because of all the clients. He didn't mind, he told her. He knew that things would settle down.

"Things go in cycles," Dan said one week before he died.

Bizzy always felt lucky that she had a husband who supported and loved her no matter what she did. She had been a forensic photographer when she and Dan McCarthy met at the party of a mutual friend. Dan was a tall, broad-shouldered hunk of a man. He couldn't take his eyes off of Bizzy. They spoke for hours at the party, pretty much ignoring the other guests. Before the evening was over, Dan asked Bizzy out on a date.

She knew when she went home that night that Dan was the one. It didn't take long for Bizzy to fall deeply in love with his easy smile, his tussle of brown hair, and most of all his big heart, which filled his lumberjack-sized chest. Just four months after they met, Dan proposed.

Diana, Bizzy's mother, was thrilled. Her father, Quint Devlin, chuckled. "I'll believe it when I'm walking you down the aisle."

"What if I elope?"

Her father laughed, "If I don't see it, I don't believe it."

A year later, he walked her down the aisle, which was more like a little path made between two rows of chairs on the beach, but he walked her. Quint had cried.

"Daddy, are those tears of joy?" Bizzy asked.

"Tears of relief," Quint said. "I just wanted you to have someone in your life that you could depend on. Of my kids, you're the one that I've always worried about. A lot."

"Ha," she said. "You were afraid I'd move back home."

"That, too," he said. They both laughed.

At Dan's funeral, Quint, an army veteran, federal agent, and chief of security at a major hospital, could hardly hold it together. Later, she heard him weeping in the bathroom of her house - a sound that haunted her.

Bizzy felt lost without Dan. Once she had made a serious blunder working a high-profile forensics case, and a killer had gotten off because of it. Bizzy wanted to quit. She told Dan that she wanted to own her own studio and take photos of *live* people. Not dead. Not mangled. Not murdered by evil people. "If you want to quit," Dan told her, "that's fine. Really. Just make sure that you really want to do the portraits and that you won't miss crime scene investigation. Your attention to detail and hunger for justice makes you really good at that. You have a passion for it."

"Not anymore," she told him. Dan wrapped her in his arms as she cried.

Bizzy did leave the department and started her own photography studio. She had kept her own name, Devlin, when they married, because even before meeting Dan she had a side gig doing portraits under her name.

Dan didn't care whether or not she took his last name. "Biz, you'll always be my missus," he said, pretending to have a strong Boston accent. "Always."

When she started portrait photography full time, Dan's support and encouragement were steadfast. "You're such a good photographer. You make people feel good about themselves. That's your gift, Bizzy." She always took great comfort in his words, though now there were times when Bizzy wished she could turn off the "Dan channel" in her head.

Now Bizzy needed to have renovations done to her house. She and Dan had talked about them before he died, and together they had saved some money for the updates. But she would need more money to complete them, and knew she had to start shooting again in her own studio. Dan would want her to. He believed in her.

LUIGI LICKED his mommy's hand and made a soft whining sound. That shook Bizzy from her reminiscing. She patted his head, "Ok, little guy. I'm going."

It took enormous strength of will for Bizzy to turn the key in the ignition and put the car in gear. *Just do it.* She pulled out of the parking spot with the dog straddling the car's center console, his head resting on Bizzy's lap.

Pullen Pointe, or "The Pointe" as locals knew it, was a one-road-in, one-road-out town. In really big storms the road sometimes flooded, and the town would be cut off from the rest of the world. In summer the Pointe was crowded, since everyone from Boston wanted a nearby spot to enjoy the beach and hang out.

Now that summer was pretty much over, the streets were no longer crowded. Bizzy drove past the public landing. The road opened up to a spectacular view of Boston. She passed the cove, and five minutes later arrived at the studio in the center of town. She parked behind the building and spotted Jacko's car. Jacko had a penchant for being late, though he was getting better. *Glad you're on time.* She didn't want to walk into an empty studio.

The back door was locked when she tried it. Usually if one of them were in the studio, the door would be unlocked. Her back stiffened. When she was a forensic photographer, she had seen a lot of not-so-good things. Doors that were normally unlocked now were locked, or vice versa, and made her think something might be amiss. She juggled her keys and the dog's leash, making as much noise as possible, and finally opened the door. The little kitchenette near the back door was littered with takeout boxes and empty water bottles. *Strange.*

She moved some boxes out of the way that blocked the door, and Luigi clung to her. *Something is off here.* As she walked further into the studio, memories started flooding back to her. She saw Dan renovating the place. It had been an old salon. But in fixing up the place she had discovered that the drop ceilings hid a beautiful beamed ceiling. Dan saw the look on Bizzy's face when she found those beams. So, over the course of several weekends, he removed the drop ceiling, patched, sanded, painted, and fixed whatever needed to be fixed. When it was finished, he presented it to her.

She looked up at her white-beamed ceilings for a long time. She smiled a big smile and said, "I'm in love."

"Any chance some of that is *for me?*" Dan asked. And she rushed into his arms. "It's *all* for you." She gave him a big kiss, and then she looked back up at the ceiling. "Hmmm... maybe half for you, half for the ceiling." She looked at the ceiling again. "Not gonna lie - a quarter for you --"

"Stop!" He laughed. "I have no idea what fraction you might go down to, but I don't want to know." Dan tickled Bizzy until she rolled to the floor in laughter.

That night was a good night. Today the pain in her heart, a stinging, throbbing pain, came back as the memories flooded in.

Bizzy walked toward the wardrobe room, which doubled as a dressing room for clients. There were boxes and trash bags cluttering the hallway.

Need to clean this up.

Bizzy noticed the wardrobe light on, and there was a stack of packages on the floor. Bizzy walked in to investigate, but a noise came from the main studio. She stopped, listened.

Snoring.

Loud snoring, with a big snort at the end.

Luigi barked when he heard the snort. The snoring grew louder. Luigi barked louder, and Bizzy heard a rustling sound and a thump on the floor. She walked in to the main studio to see Jacko, half-dressed and sitting on the floor beside an ornate settee. His dark brown hair was all over the place, in full bed-head display. He pushed it to one side, but a few short hairs stuck out despite his best efforts. Bizzy saw all this in a mirror as she walked into the main studio. At that moment, Jacko saw her and jumped up.

"Bizzy? You're here. You're early."

"No," said Bizzy, "I'm on time to prep for the shoot."

She scanned the studio. Near the front, a picture window opened to the street. The space donned a white seamless backdrop on one side and different colored cloth backdrops on the other side, all rigged for easy changing to suit each client. Around the periphery of the studio, other equipment, stools, and props stood ready.

The lighting equipment was set up the way she liked it. Two strobe lights faced the cloth backdrops, with a third light pointing to the backdrops themselves. Dan had created a beauty center for the studio, a makeup table with lights all around a mirror. Now, though, there were men's grooming products strewn across the table. And there were sheets and a blanket on the elegant settee they often used for shoots.

"What's going on, Jacko?" Bizzy asked, as she took it all in. *Jacko slept here?*

She loved the studio and needed it now more than ever. She had to get the finances back on track, especially since she was going to renovate the house. Besides, even on her darkest day, when her sadness about Dan took over, she didn't have the heart to get rid of it because they had put so much time and effort into this studio to make it her place. Dan *wanted* her to be here.

"I didn't know you were going to be here this early," Jacko said. He was wearing boxer shorts. There was disarray underneath the settee. A suitcase had clothes hanging out, and there were some plastic trash bags with more clothes. Clearly he had not prepared for her early arrival.

"Jacko, we have an appointment today - remember?"

"Yeah, I thought... I thought..." Jacko stammered. "I thought I was coming to your house to pick you up."

"You said we were meeting here."

"Oh, okay. All right." He wrapped a blanket around

himself and stood up. Jacko clearly was not fully awake yet as he stumbled around, reaching for his clothes.

"Are you *sleeping* here?" Bizzy asked. She looked Jacko over in his unkempt state, his hair sticking up, out of place.

"Have you seen my glasses?" Jacko asked, evading the question.

Bizzy took the glasses from a stool and handed them to him.

"I just needed somewhere to stay for a few days," Jacko finally answered, cleaning and then adjusting his glasses on his face.

"I'm pretty sure the studio rental contract says that nobody can *live* here," Bizzy said.

Jacko started hemming and hawing, "Yeah, I know, I know, but..."

Bizzy put her hand up and stopped him. "Jacko, just tell me what's going on."

"Well..." He didn't look at her. "Marissa and I are no longer together."

Bizzy stepped back a little bit. "Wow." She thought Jacko and Marissa would eventually break up, but didn't know it would be so soon.

"Are you going to ask me why?" Jacko took his jeans and tried to put them on while he was wrapped in the blanket. He put one leg in and toppled back onto the couch.

"Forget the blanket, just put your jeans on. I've just seen you in your boxer shorts," Bizzy said.

Jacko dropped the blanket, stood up again, and finished putting on his jeans. *He had the perfect bed-head look.* Jacko was a little vain when it came to his looks, especially his hair.

"Why?" Bizzy whispered.

"She decided she didn't like me anymore," said Jacko.

He started folding the blanket and the other bedding that had been on the couch. His crumpled clothes hung on him loosely, and Bizzy realized that he had lost weight.

"What do you mean, she decided that she didn't *like* you?" Her question had a hint of anger in it.

"Just that: She decided she didn't like me. She packed my bags, and she left them here. I'm just glad I was here. Otherwise they could have been..." His voice drifted.

"You didn't have any say in it? Isn't it your house, too?" Bizzy asked, now letting her anger pepper every word.

"It's not actually *my* house. Well, I mean, we weren't married, Bizzy, and the house is in her name. So legally she had the right to kick me out."

"You guys have been together for so long." Bizzy took a deep breath. She watched Jacko fidget with the blankets and bedding now expertly folded. He placed them in a box and put them away.

"We've been together for three years or so. But you know, this last year we've been kind of arguing a lot."

She nodded. She did know that. *All the time.*

He sighed heavily and walked toward the bathroom. She followed him part way and could hear the water running. She heard him splashing water on his face.

"Why now?" Bizzy called in to him.

"She said I wasn't bringing in enough money. And, frankly, she's right about that. I was trying to keep *this* going." He walked out of the bathroom with a towel in hand and motioned to the studio.

Bizzy put her head down. "You've been helping me." She went over to one of the lights. She moved it to one side. "I'm sure she didn't like you spending so much time with me." Bizzy and Jacko were almost the same age, with Jacko being a few months younger. Marissa, on the other hand, was five years younger. She also was a successful real estate agent in Boston.

When Dan died, Jacko helped Bizzy not just with the business but with anything she needed, from trash removal to snow shoveling. Jacko now knew all her neighbors, and, for the most part, they liked him and he liked them. Edy, a beautiful African American flight attendant in her early 50s, loved him, because Jacko constantly flirted with her. He was good flirt, but he didn't stray from Marissa. Bizzy knew how much he wanted that relationship to work.

"Marissa didn't especially care for me spending so much time here. But she was kind of seeing someone else too, you know. Not that we are seeing..."

"Too?" asked Bizzy incredulously.

"She thought something was going on with me and you, but I think it's because she *wanted* something to be going on. That way she could have indignation and support from all her friends." He went back into the bathroom in the back of the studio and started brushing his teeth. His electric toothbrush was loud. He was meticulous about his teeth, and the brushing went on for a full two minutes.

All Bizzy could do was shake her head. "I had no idea this was going on. No idea. I'm so sorry."

"You've been kind of in a fog, Bizzy. It's kind of been a weird thing. I've been doing a lot of shoots, so we've been paying the rent and the bills. But I haven't necessarily paid myself."

"Well that's not right. You've got to pay yourself." Back in the studio, she pulled equipment out and set up a tripod.

"You're right, I have to pay myself. So I'm glad to see that you're here, and we're going to get the business back on track." Jacko walked back into the studio. He walked over to the make-up station and grimaced in the mirror. He picked up a tube of hair gel, spread a dab onto his hair, and combed it. He smiled into the mirror. "Hi, handsome," he said to his reflection.

Bizzy laughed. "Keep telling yourself that." One thing that hadn't changed was the good-natured banter that was part and parcel of Bizzy and Jacko's relationship over the years. Bizzy was grateful for that.

He walked over and joined her in the middle of the studio.

I missed this place. "We *are* going to get it back on track. And maybe change some things. I am going to get out of my fog." She turned to him. "I'm really sorry about Marissa. I know you wanted it to work."

He smiled at her. He had that smile that made most women's hearts go pitter-patter. And those blue eyes. *Loving* eyes. She was used to it now, so her heart didn't pitter or patter. *That* much. Dan had kidded her when Jacko came on board at the studio. "You got the handsome Italian guy as your assistant."

"Not as handsome as you, Baby," she said to Dan with a kiss.

"I know," Dan said. "I'm not worried." Dan never did.

Now Jacko and Bizzy had been working together for years. And Jacko and Dan had liked each other. Bizzy teased Dan that he liked Jacko better than he liked her. "Nope," he said. "He's a good friend to me, and a better one to you."

She stared at Jacko, watching him adjust the white seamless backdrop. *He's taken over the business. For me.* "I would have gone under if not for you."

He strode over to where they kept dresses and other various clothing for shoots. She could see that he had hung up a few of his shirts and pants. He picked out a pair of dress pants and a shirt. "Be right back, boss." And he went into the dressing room.

He came back out a minute later, his clothes smooth and sharp. His dark, brown hair was now perfectly coiffed.

"You did all this," she motioned to his body, "in less than two minutes?"

He smiled that smile again. She rolled her eyes.

"It's impressive, huh?"

She laughed. "What time are the Thompsons coming in?"

"At 10:30, and it's just the mother and daughter. And they said they didn't want a makeup / hair person."

"Yeah, well they own a beauty salon. I'm sure Betsy is quite good at that."

Luigi had been kind of quiet all this time, but suddenly, he stretched, whined, and did a Chewbacca-type sound.

"Uh oh! Catch him, Jacko!"

The dog was now over in a corner sniffing. He then went into a little squat. "Oh my. Luigi. No. No!" She grabbed him and picked him up, but there was a little puddle on the floor. It was close to Jacko's backpack with his laptop in it.

Jacko moved the backpack quickly, retrieved a roll of paper towels, and started to wipe up Luigi's gift to the studio.

"You don't have to do that."

"Bizzy, I've basically been squatting here, so I don't mind cleaning up." He sprayed some floor cleaner on the spot, and wiped it up.

"He is potty trained at home." Bizzy patted the dog on the head.

"Looks like we'll have to potty train him here, too."

While Jacko finished straightening up the studio,

Bizzy took the pup outside, where he looked up at her with questioning eyes. "Not clear why we're out here, Little Guy?" She squatted down to him. "You are so cute, Luigi. Finish doing your business . I need to shoot your portrait."

When she came back in, Jacko was setting up the camera. "Jacko, We're adding pet photography to our list of portraits," Bizzy said.

"But you only liked dogs. Pets are more than just dogs." He clicked the shutter to test the lights. They flashed, and Luigi jumped.

"I like *some* cats. My mom has a cat."

Jacko laughed. "You only like the cats that *act* like dogs. You said Cranky-"

"That's not his real name. Fin Barr is his real name. He's just always cranky."

She picked up the camera. Luigi was sitting in front of a backdrop, right in front of the settee. She picked Luigi up and put him on the settee. "Sit, Luigi." He sat up and looked at her. She took a photo. Luigi barked when the strobe went off but didn't move. She went up to Luigi and gave him a treat. He laid down. "Sit." He sat back up. She snapped again. He barked again. She gave him another treat. "I think you're getting the hang of this, Little Guy!"

She glanced around the studio. "Yeah, Jacko, let's put something on social media. Maybe just FB or Instagram. Put it on Tuesday, Wednesday. And boost it for this area. Say 'Building portfolio, free portrait'. Even if it's just a couple of owners and pets show up, we can start our portfolio."

"I'll need a photo for the post," Jacko said.

Luigi barked at a person peering through the big window.

"I think we have our model," Jacko said. "Should we send something out by snail mail?"

"Nah, let's get a couple of shoots under our belt first."

Jacko smiled. "Now we're talking, Bizzy Devlin."

She pulled the camera up to take another photo of Luigi on the settee. "Sit." He sat up, and she took the photo.

Yup, that felt good.

CHAPTER THREE

Around 10:30 a.m. the front door opened, and Betsy Thompson and her daughter, Carson, walked in. They saw Luigi and immediately cooed at him.

"He is *so* cute," Carson giggled.

"Adorable," said Betsy.

A little squeak came from Betsy's bag, and Bizzy realized that Betsy had a little furry thing in her purse, under her arm.

"Who's that?" Luigi jumped from the settee, sniffing at Betsy's elbow for the furry object.

Betsy brought the fluffball up to her nose. In a high-pitched voice she said, "This little honey is Buster."

When Carson saw the question on Bizzy's face, she clarified, "This is the *new* Buster."

"You know I can't live without a dog," Betsy said. She kept the little fluffball near her nose. "And this little Buster is just the remedy for a broken heart."

Bizzy smiled. This wasn't the first, or even the second, Buster. And most likely not the last. All her Busters were Pomeranians. And they all went everywhere with her, even to her hair salon where they scampered around, usually to the delight of the clients.

"Luigi, stop jumping at Buster." Bizzy grabbed Luigi by the collar and pulled him toward her.

Carson sneered a little, "It's the third Buster I can remember, but I know she had Busters before me."

Betsy said, "They've all been great dogs." She gave a snide glance over to her daughter, bordering on sarcastic, "Just like my teenage daughter is...great."

Luigi wrangled himself out of Bizzy's grasp and jumped up to try to smell the fluffball. He almost got to him, but Betsy pulled the little Pomeranian away. She pulled out a little baggy with treats. "Luigi, how old are you? You are a puppy, aren't you? I'm not sure Buster wants to play. He's a little older than you." She winked at Luigi. "Maybe in a little while." She slipped Luigi a treat, which he wolfed down eagerly.

Most of the time no one knew the age of the dogs Betsy adopted over the years. Betsy would get attached, and three or four years later something would happen, and a new Buster would come into the Thompson house. They were all well-loved dogs.

Carson rolled her eyes and said in huff, "He's probably going to be visiting the rainbow bridge sooner rather than later."

"Don't say that!" Betsy said to her daughter.

Carson, at seventeen, was not much interested in her mother's good deeds at rescuing Pomeranians. "I wish we'd get a *different* type of dog at least. Something bigger, and pretty. Like Luigi." Luigi kept an eye on the furball Betsy cradled.

Bizzy looked over to Jacko, who was smiling. "Hey

Betsy, I'm thinking about getting into pet portraiture. What do you think?"

"That's a great idea!" Betsy replied. Carson gagged a little. "In fact, why don't you take Buster's photo instead of this one's senior pictures?"

"Mooooom!"

Bizzy laughed. "Carson, did you bring a couple of outfits?"

Carson lifted a plastic bag, bulging with clothes.

"Great!" Bizzy didn't normally see clients present their wardrobe this way, but she knew with teenagers to expect anything.

Carson proceeded to pull out one outfit after another and laid them on the settee. Each piece of clothing had less material then the last.

Bizzy pointed to the back of the studio. "The changing room is back there. Also, there are plenty of other dress options on the rack. Feel free to try something on if it catches your eye."

"They're separated by size," Jacko called out to her.

Carson stuffed the clothes back in the plastic bag and walked toward the dressing room, her overflowing bag of clothes rustling as she went by Jacko.

Betsy turned her head away from Buster. "I paid a lot of money for those scraps of clothing, and she doesn't even take care of them." She pulled Buster to her face, and gave him a bunch of little kisses. Buster, on his part, gave Betsy one little kiss. "Is that all I get, Buster? Don't be stingy."

It didn't take long for Carson to come out in her first outfit. Betsy handed Buster to Carson. "Can you hold him a minute while mommy does her tinky-tink?" Carson took the dog, rolling her eyes again. *You know kid, your eyes might just get stuck if you keep rolling them.* Bizzy smiled.

Then she saw Carson and Buster together. "Carson, can you stand right there, please?" She pointed to the center point in front of the backdrop. Carson moved to the spot as directed. "Look here." She looked toward Bizzy. "Now pull the dog up to your face and give him a little snuggle."

Carson was a natural model. A lot of teenage girls were these days, since they followed the beautiful and the glamorous on social media. Bizzy was sure the outfit Carson wore, a kerchief triangle exposing one shoulder, could be found somewhere on one of the sites. She snapped.

"Turn forty-five degrees toward the light." Bizzy showed her how to do the pose. Carson mirrored Bizzy and moved as she was directed. The dog's cute face rested on Carson's shoulder. Click.

Carson flashed her perfect pearly-whites. Buster didn't mind the flash like Luigi had. Luigi barked for him.

"Sssh, Luigi," Jacko said.

Bizzy had Carson rotate and continued shooting at slightly different angles. "A little more," she said. And Carson turned again.

"Now look back over your shoulder toward the camera." Carson took the direction like a pro.

Betsy came out of the bathroom and watched the photo shoot as it progressed. "I love it!"

Carson and Buster were nuzzling their noses. Bizzy took a couple more shots. Jacko called over to her. "What are your settings?"

It was a normal question many assistants asked their photographer bosses, but it was also their code phrase to remind Bizzy to have the client change outfits, or for them to change to a different background. As a photographer, Bizzy got lost in the moment and could easily shoot more than 200 photos with the same backdrop and outfit.

Bizzy glanced down to the back of her camera. "Okay, Carson, why don't you get into your next outfit?"

Carson handed the dog back to her mother and went to the dressing room in the back of the studio. This particular photo package included three outfits, and Bizzy expected the next one to be even skimpier than the one she had been wearing.

"They are really cute, Betz." Bizzy showed her the back of the camera.

"Oh, Buster is adorable."

"Um, your daughter is in the photo, too," Bizzy reminded her.

"Yeah, but I'm going to bust on her a little bit. She's been a little witchy lately."

"Okay, but please do it *after* I finish taking the photos."

Betsy laughed. Carson came back out. This time Carson wore one of the dresses from the wardrobe room. It was a deep red chiffon evening gown, sleeveless, with a v-neck and crisscross back. It was flowy and hung off Carson perfectly.

"Wow, Carson, you look fantastic in that dress!" Bizzy said.

She twirled. "I love it."

"Maybe she can wear that to prom?" Betsy said.

"No, Mom, I know exactly what I am wearing."

Bizzy snapped as Carson twirled, and Jacko silently adjusted the main light to follow Carson's movements. "Follow me with your eyes," Bizzy said. "Head and shoulder..."

Bizzy hardly noticed at the time, but she was starting to lose herself once more in the joy of a good photo shoot.

～

AFTER BIZZY FINISHED PHOTOGRAPHING Carson in her final outfit, mother and daughter got ready to leave. Carson now wanted to hold the dog. Betsy winked at Bizzy, "I may bring Buster in for his own shoot. That way he won't be so distracted. And Bizzy, if you want my two cents worth, do the pet photography. I know you will get a ton of clients. And I'll put Buster's photo in my salon."

Bizzy and Jacko thanked her and smiled. Betsy and Carson walked to their car with little Buster. Jacko looked down at his watch. "Not bad, Biz. Only an hour. I hope there aren't too many shots to edit."

Bizzy went and sat on the settee, and Luigi jumped up on it next to her. She sighed.

"You okay?" asked Jacko.

"Yeah. Yes. It felt good."

"What?"

She motioned around her. "This. Shooting. Being back in the studio." She reached down and stroked Luigi.

"You were in the zone, Biz. Totally focused. Working your creative magic. It was good to see you like that again."

Bizzy smiled. "Jacko, you said that we need to do some planning for the business. Now we have to think of different marketing strategies."

"Our web page and all the social media stuff hasn't been updated in months." He said it delicately.

"It's okay, Jacko. I know I've been out of it." She turned her head away so he couldn't see her tears forming. "We can hire someone to do it, right? Isn't that what you said?"

Jacko nodded. "I have someone who will help out. She's a 22-year old who eventually wants to do social media for clients full time. She's thinking of Bizzy Devlin Photography as a stepping stone and offered to do our work at a great price."

"That sounds great, Jacko."

Luigi walked around the studio sniffing. With a leap he jumped up the settee. Jacko picked up the camera and pressed the shutter to take his picture. The lights popped. He barked but preened a little this time.

"He's so damn cute!" Bizzy squealed.

"I know, Bizzy." He squatted down. Jacko snapped his fingers, and Luigi looked over. "He's, like, a totally adorable teddy bear."

Every time Luigi went to get up, Bizzy rushed in with a treat, and he sat back down. Jacko kept taking photos.

Bizzy stroked Luigi behind his ears. "Jacko, we could take pictures of, you know, just really cute animals."

He stood there for a moment and looked at Luigi. "I'm not sure that's how it works."

Bizzy grabbed the camera from him. "It will. I know people take pictures of their own pets, but we could really make something of it." Jacko watched as she went around Luigi. She would give him a treat, and he'd do what she wanted. Bizzy giggled every time he did a funny face. Jacko stared at her. Bizzy hadn't really felt that kind of excitement in a long time. "Jacko, we can actually get into it. Every pet owner wants photos of their pets."

Jacko watched the spark in Bizzy coming alive again. "You know, Biz," he said, going around and turning some lights off, "we *could* get into it." Jacko had gone to one of the finest photography schools in the country. "Ok. I'm in. Let's do pet portraits!"

"You excited?" she asked.

"You realize that you will have to photograph cats, right?"

She nodded.

He smiled. "And there are a lot of cats in this world that don't act like dogs. Like...most of them."

Bizzy picked up a broom and held it in the air as if it were a royal scepter. "Bring on the most diva-like, queenie cat."

"Why do I know I'm the one who is going to get scratched?"

Bizzy squatted on the floor and held out her hands to Luigi. "Come." He jumped off and ran into her arms, then licked her face all over. "Good boy." She picked him up and buried her face in his fur.

Bizzy turned to Jacko. "Jacko, if you need a place to stay, you can stay in my spare bedroom as long as you need to...or want."

Jacko put his head down. Bizzy clearly saw that he was moved by the gesture. "Thank you," he said.

"Yeah, you can't really stay here. The rental agreement says no living in the studio."

He nodded.

She looked over at him. "Then it's settled."

CHAPTER FOUR

Bizzy and Luigi ran up the boardwalk. She stood in front of the cottage and looked it up and down. The home that she and Dan had shared would no longer be the same. Sadness washed over her. *No crying. The house has to be fixed.* It did not honor Dan and his beloved sea cottage if it disintegrated into the sand.

She told everyone in the neighborhood that workers and equipment would rumble around, and it would get noisy for a while.

Only Schaeffer, her neighbor whose property was adjacent to hers, gave her a hard time. Bizzy had to get approval from the town conservation committee. Schaeffer showed up at the committee meeting and told them he didn't like it.

"Reasons, Mr. Schaeffer?" the chairperson had asked him.

He stood up in the cramped hearing room. "I just don't like it."

"You have to give us some reason for us even to consider your objection." The chairperson had said calmly. She, on the other hand, wanted to throttle Schaeffer.

Schaeffer glared at Bizzy and then stomped out of the hearing room. With him no longer objecting, the committee members gave their permission to renovate.

With the approval in hand, Bizzy took the plunge. Her contractor, Howie Dunlap, showed up a week later with the building permit, handed it to Bizzy, and told her to tape it in the window facing the front of the house. "Oh, and the excavating will start tomorrow." Howie then turned and walked down the boardwalk, his booted feet thudding on the wooden planks.

A pang of fear rose up in Bizzy, and she ran over to Edy's house, both excited and terrified to tell her it was starting tomorrow.

"What are they going to do?"

"Excavate first. Demolition." Then Bizzy broke down and sobbed.

"You can stay at my house if it gets to be too much." She wrapped her arms around Bizzy.

Bizzy lifted her head. "It will be all right. Howie said they would be done in two months."

Edy laughed the knowing laugh of someone who had been through a difficult renovation. "That's not the way it happens, Bizzy. Have you ever heard the saying, 'Twice as long, twice the price'?"

"Yes," Bizzy said, "but I don't have either 'twice' - the time or the money."

Edy reached out and patted her on the shoulder.

"I am excited, though," Bizzy said, breathless.

"So what else are they doing?"

"After they check the foundation to see if it needs to be strengthened, they will reinforce the frame. Then they'll replace the plumbing and electrical and put in new insulation and drywall. Open up the main floor. I have been *dying* for a new kitchen and bathroom. And if the budget stretches, some new appliances."

Edy smiled. "I'm glad you're doing it. It's a fresh start."

Bizzy went to bed early but could hardly sleep that night.

~

THE NEXT MORNING, Bizzy and Edy were both up early. Neither of them said anything when Howie and three young workers started removing the sections of the deck. Bizzy knew they were both thinking the same thing: the two guys who had built that deck were now gone - Bizzy's husband Dan was dead, and Edy's son Jay had moved south.

Luigi darted over to Edy's hostas and did a kamikaze nosedive into them. He rolled around and made sure every inch of his body was covered in hosta leaves and dirt. "No, Lou!" Bizzy cried in horror. "Get out of Aunt Edy's hostas!"

"Don't worry, Biz. I'm going to get rid of them once and for all when the renovations are done," Edy said.

Luigi, covered in dirt and hosta leaves, trotted happily back to the two women, but what looked like wood chips hung on his fur. Bizzy leaned down to pull them off. She showed Edy.

"Mulch," Edy said.

"What do you need *that* for?" Bizzy asked.

"It helps keep the plants moist." Their eyes were fixed on the young men as they worked.

"Remember how Schaeffer tried to block Dan and Jay from building the deck?" Bizzy asked.

"Yes. Oh Bertie, Bertie. And that's when he was *nice*."

"I'm having trouble remembering when he was nice."

Edy turned to her, "Biz, you have to remember that Jeannie was sick for a long time..."

"I know."

Edy moaned as one of the guys carried away some old planks. "A lot of memories go with that deck."

"I hear you," Bizzy commiserated.

Bizzy and Dan married a little over ten years ago. She loved Dan's beach cottage, but she begged Dan for a sorely needed new deck. Dan was all about pleasing his queen and set about the task.

Dan took Edy's 17-year-old son, Jay, as his helper for the project. Jay's dad and Edy had split when Jay was barely two. From that time on, Edy was a dedicated and loving single mom. But when Jay was a teen, he began staying out late more and more often, and she was worried about his choice of friends.

Dan took him under his wing and taught him a few tricks that he had learned in his amateur carpenter life. Dan told Edy that Jay was very interested and asked a lot of questions. She and Bizzy loved to see Dan and Jay working together. "He's a good kid," Dan told both Bizzy and Edy numerous times throughout the project.

"They had a good time," Bizzy now mused out loud to Edy. When the last bit of deck was now gone, all that remained was sand.

"That project changed Jay. Helped make him the carpenter he is today," Edy stood up and said. "Of course, he's doing it down in North Carolina, not my preference."

"Ever think of moving down there?" Bizzy asked.

"I have no intention of living down south. I like it here just fine. I have the sea," Edy said as she picked up an old rake that was uncovered when the boards came up. She started to rake the sand. "You feeling okay?" she asked Bizzy, as she made designs in the sand with the rake.

"Yeah," Bizzy replied. "I wonder if I have photos of them building the deck."

"Bizzy, you have photos of *everything*."

Bizzy nodded. "Yup, I probably do. I like freezing those moments."

"Yeah, girl, but don't go back to them too much." She stopped raking. "They'll freeze you."

"You're right."

"And being back in the studio, was that good?" Edy was now drawing a beautiful palm tree in the sand with the rake.

"I had a really good shoot. I also found out that Jacko is living there."

Edy looked up, surprised. "What?"

"Jacko and his girlfriend broke up, and he was living in the studio."

"He seems so nice. You can never tell with men. They seem so nice," she huffed, "but then sometimes they're not." She roughed up the sand with the rake in short bursts.

"That sounds like a woman scorned," Bizzy said, looking down at Edy's elaborate, but now ruined, design.

Edy laughed. But then she raked over her artwork. "Long time, long time. And way over it."

Bizzy giggled and said with sarcasm, "Oh yeah. Sounds like it."

Edy leaned the rake against her house. "Dan would like that you're doing this."

"Dan would like it, 'cause it means the house isn't falling down," Bizzy said.

"Dan would like it, because he always wanted to see you happy and well taken care of," Edy replied.

Bizzy sat on a plastic beach chair that sunk a bit into the sand. "I told Jacko he could live here until he finds a new place."

"How long do you think?" Edy asked.

"Don't know." Luigi came over and nuzzled up to Bizzy. She patted him and rubbed his ears, and she wiped away some of the dirt and mulch. "I think his sweet spot is behind his ears."

"Jacko's?" Edy laughed.

"Very funny. No, Luigi's."

"I know," Edy said. "Are you worried what people will think?"

Bizzy made her own design in the sand with her foot. "No," said Bizzy. "Only you."

"Just don't get attached."

"What does that mean?"

"Well, he's your assistant, and now he's going to be your housemate."

"No, he will be a tenant. A boarder."

Edy shook her head. "Well, he will be sharing your house. And your renovations are about to start."

"I thought he might be able to help with that. Do the 'man speak' thing when Howie tries to throw stuff at me." They watched as Luigi ran around the sandy yard.

Edy got up. "I'm getting another cup of sludge. Want one?"

Bizzy nodded.

≈

WHEN THE DECK was completely removed, a small front-end loader came rumbling up the boardwalk.

The man steering the Bobcat bulged out of the seat, and

Bizzy laughed. Edy came to the door when the whirring sound of the machine came closer. It looked old, and the paint was chipped.

"And so it begins..." Edy came out of her door and stood there, watching.

"It's a kiddie-size front-end loader." Bizzy and Edy both laughed.

"Maybe they should consider making one for bigger kids, 'cause that guy does *not* fit in this one." Edy motioned to the driver of the Bobcat.

Once they could see past the machine, they realized Howie and another man were behind it.

"That's the structural engineer guy." Bizzy pointed to a 30ish man in construction boots, jeans, and flannel shirt. He had aviator sunglasses. *Yeah, you're cool.*

"That man is a GQ model," huffed Edy. "A little too young for me. You should ask him to take his model photos."

Bizzy laughed. "I know, right? He looks like he could be good with his hands."

Edy started making little purring sounds.

"Okay, stop it now. He knows we're looking at him," Bizzy said.

"I'm going back into the house. It's steamy out here." Edy walked back in her own house but stayed at her screen door.

The little machine began to move the sand away from the foundation. After a few minutes of digging, the action halted, and the Bobcat guy turned it off. "We need to dig this next part by hand," Howie announced.

Luigi barked in the house and ran from window to window.

"Howie, can I bring him out for a sec?" Bizzy asked.

"Sure," Howie said.

Edy hadn't strayed far from her screen door. "Bring him

over here, Biz. I'll keep him company." Bizzy went in the house, grabbed the leash, and quickly put it on Luigi.

Bizzy watched a couple of workers dig near the base of her house. Luigi barked from Edy's door. *My little guy just wants to play.*

"Shhh, Luigi, shhhh." Edy smoothed down Luigi's apricot-colored crown of hair.

"Hold it!" Howie said. He turned to the guy sitting in the Bobcat. "Jimmy, can you get back in there?"

The Bobcat driver turned the machine back on, shattering the silence with its rumbling. It moved closer to the house, scooping out the sand that had surrounded Bizzy's cottage for a century.

Howie put up his hand, and the driver stopped. Now the GQ model/structural engineer moved to see the hole. He also pulled out his phone and took a few photos.

"Need anything else here?" Howie asked.

GQ guy said something, but Bizzy didn't hear it over the noise of the machine and Luigi's barking.

"You want me to take him for a walk, Biz?" Edy had Luigi's leash in her hand. Bizzy nodded.

Edy carefully brought the dog out, holding him tight so he wouldn't go close to the new hole or the machine.

"Thanks, Edy." Bizzy waved to her dog as he went toward the beach. Luigi reluctantly went with Edy, but he kept turning back, pulling hard to be with Bizzy.

The men started the process all over again at the next corner of the house, and with each new scoop of the machine, more of the sandy ground seemed to dislodge. It felt like a small earthquake. Over on Edy's side of the property, a couple of potted plants fell over.

Howie put his hand up again. The Bobcat stopped. The guys got in there with shovels, and finally the structural engineer got in to take photos of this section of the foundation. He went over to Howie. Howie nodded. They all had very serious looks. Bizzy smelled more money burning from her bank account.

Howie glanced over to her, smiled, and put his thumb up.

"What does that mean, Howie?"

"Artie here," he pointed to GQ guy, "says everything is good. We'll fortify it for the stairs and porch, but what's here is solid."

GQ's name is Artie. And she nodded to Howie.

"We're going to go get a coffee, and then we will be back in about 20 minutes."

The Bobcat driver pulled back and then started to move the machine toward the main boardwalk. Everything seemed to rattle as it went by. Things fell over. Even the sand on Edy's side of the shared area between the houses shifted.

Off they all went - the Bobcat driver, and the workers who were standing around watching. As they were leaving, Bizzy heard Artie ask, "Where are we going?"

They all scoffed at him. "Break time."

Edy passed them with the dog. As soon as Luigi saw Bizzy again, he started pulling on the leash to get to her. "You can let him go." He ran to Bizzy and started to jump on her.

"It seems like they worked for about 20 minutes," Edy shook her head. "And now they are breaking for an hour. This is a job with a lot of breaks."

"Looks that way, doesn't it?"

Edy shook her head and looked down the boardwalk. "We should put out some beach chairs for this. Maybe if they think that we're watching, they'll work harder and longer."

"Or we *could* just aggravate them by doing that," Bizzy said, watching Luigi zoom around in the newly uncovered sand.

"I just put some chairs away," Edy said. "You think I will tempt fate with a hurricane if I take them out?"

"Nah, I think you put them away a little too early, anyway." Bizzy laughed.

They sat on the chairs and watched Luigi run around and around. Occasionally he'd stop, dig out a new hole in the hosta patch, and stick his belly in it. Then, after two seconds, he'd get up and run around and dig another hole in a different spot.

"We need to fill those holes up before they get back," said Bizzy.

Edy nodded.

They both stared at the place where the deck had been. Neither woman said anything. Bizzy saw Dan and Jay there, like a movie flashback.

She heard their laughter and an occasional "working word," as Dan liked to refer to cussing, echoing between the houses.

"What are your plans when...I don't know...when you finish high school?" Dan had asked Jay. "Are you off to college?"

"I like computers," Jay said, "But once I graduate from high school, I'm done with school."

Dan talked to him of different options, including the military.

"No chance. Living with my mom has been way too close to being in the military." Jay laughed.

Dan, Jay, and that day were frozen in Bizzy's memory.

Right now, when she looked in this place, she saw Dan looking at her, winking, their eyes meeting. Then he faded.

"What the heck is that dog doing?" Edy got out of her chair.

"What?" Bizzy said, startled, and saw that Luigi was digging at the far corner of Edy's house with gusto. Edy's hostas, now in shreds, were flying all over the sand. Luigi was digging faster and faster, like Wyle E. Coyote on steroids.

Sand now flew everywhere. "Maybe there's a bone or something there." Bizzy jumped up and ran for the dog. "Or worse, a dead skunk."

The hostas lay all over the place in tatters, and Luigi kept digging. Sand, dirt, and plants flew everywhere, hitting Bizzy as she got closer. She got to the dog and pulled him back.

"Oh Edy, I'm so sorry." Luigi strained at his collar to get back at whatever he was digging for.

Edy picked up the plant leaves, "Hostas don't die," she waved the plant at the dog, "unless a ferocious puppy is at work. That's okay LuLu. Aunt Edy is going to plant something else there, anyway."

Bizzy snapped the leash back on the dog. "Luigi, sit." Her commands were in vain this time, because Luigi just kept going for the hole he had dug.

"I am not going to look at what's there," Edy said, stepping back.

"I guess I have to," said Bizzy, "since my dog did the damage. Will you hold him?" She handed the leash to Edy. "Say you're sorry, Luigi, for digging up all the horrible hostas."

Bizzy stepped carefully towards the hole, shut her eyes,

and then opened them. "I don't smell anything, so it's not a dead skunk."

She gingerly took a step and could see something in the remains of the plants. She squatted and then leaned in and moved the leaves. At first her eyes couldn't believe it. "Hey Edy, do you have any Halloween decorations you're missing?"

"I don't decorate for Halloween," Edy said. "You know me. I don't even give candy out anymore. Kids these days are only satisfied with the big candy bars."

"So you never had, like, skeleton decorations or anything?" Bizzy asked.

"No, Biz, that's just creepy. Halloween is not my thing."

Bizzy cleared away a little sand. What stared back at her was a skull. She brushed away some more sand with her hand. And then she saw that the skull had arms and a rib cage, and attached to the rib cage was a black tattered rag.

CHAPTER FIVE

"Call 9-1-1!" Bizzy said as she grabbed Luigi and ran into her house. Her camera was on the counter, left there from that morning's sunrise shoot. She rushed over to her camera bag and pulled out a flash and a ruler.

"Why am I calling 9-1-1?" Edy shrieked.

"Tell them we've found some human remains," Bizzy said grimly.

"Yes, Pullen Pointe Police? My friend said to call you." Edy's voice was shaky. "Apparently we have some, some...human remains."

Bizzy ran back to where the skeleton lay and methodically began to take pictures. *Follow the process, Biz: wide shots, mid-range, and close ups. Get the scale, and shoot from all angles,* Bizzy told herself, repeating what she had learned in her training as a forensic photographer. She shot first without flash, then with it. She set a ruler next to the skeleton, beginning with the skull. She squatted down, taking a nearby stick and gently moving some debris that the dog had deposited there as he dug. She walked around the bones in a circle, shooting and frequently checking the camera screen to make sure the photos were well exposed and in focus. She noticed what looked like a lighter hanging from what was a partially disintegrated pocket. Bizzy knew better than to touch the lighter, but got some close-up photos of it.

Bizzy and Edy could hear the approaching laughter of Howie and the other workers coming back from their coffee break. Bizzy heard their work boots in a weird, almost march-like unison on the boardwalk.

"Stop them from coming in, Edy!" Bizzy commanded.

A faint siren sounded in the distance as the men rounded the corner of the house. Edy blocked their way.

"Can't come in here right now, fellas," she stammered.

Howie stepped forward. "Why not? I'm paying a guy a lot of money to dig today."

Bizzy came from the corner of Edy's house, camera bobbing in front of her. "The Bobcat jogged something loose in the sand near Edy's house."

"No way," said Howie, peering around Bizzy. "We've been super careful. You know I'm all about safety. And we got our clearance from 'Dig Safe' for all the utilities."

"I know Howie," said Bizzy. "Apparently it's something that's been there a long time, and the dog helped uncover it even more."

Luigi's little face peered out the window. He barked in a low, rhythmic way.

Now they could all hear the sirens. Luigi barked again.

"Guys, it seems there are some human bones over there." Bizzy pointed to the corner of the house.

"How do you know it's not some animal or something?" Howie asked.

"For starters, because he or she is wearing - or *was* wearing - clothes," said Bizzy.

The youngest of the helpers stepped back and turned away. "Oh, yuck. Oh, that is not cool."

Tinker, the smaller guy, said, "You scared, Robbie?"

Luigi yelped again. Now the chorus of sirens stopped and was replaced by some shouting down at the end of the boardwalk.

"Police are here," Tinker said.

Vibrations thundered from several heavy-footed people on the boardwalk. EMTs, fire fighters, Pullen Pointe patrolmen, state police, and two detectives arrived on the scene quickly. Radios sounded as the first officer arrived.

"The remains are over there," Bizzy pointed, and several of them went in the direction of the body.

Bizzy recognized Officer Castelli, who approached her. "Bizzy, can you take me through what happened here?" He wrote down her statement as Bizzy explained about the renovations and digging, and how Luigi found the body.

From inside the house, Luigi peered out the windows, moving from window to window, barking louder from inside the house as more people arrived.

More heavy footsteps came up the boardwalk. Then the noise died down as all the emergency personnel stopped moving around. Bizzy heard a single set of footsteps with a familiar cadence.

Detective Doug Williams made a commanding entrance. And unlike the other two detectives mulling about, who wore simple business casual clothing, Doug Williams wore a suit and tie. He stood ramrod straight, and immediately the other two detectives turned to acknowledge him. Bizzy knew he was in charge. Doug and Dan had been friends since their days together at Boston College High School. And Doug had been a pallbearer at Dan's funeral. Bizzy also knew Doug from working with him as forensic photographer on several cases where he was lead investigator.

Doug nodded to Bizzy when he saw her, but walked right over to the body without stopping. One of the other detectives, a short guy with a blazer that didn't quite match his pants, followed Williams to the body. The sand shifted a little and started to sink back into the hole with the body.

"Careful, Sullivan," Williams ordered. "You're going to destroy the crime scene."

"Yes, Sergeant," Sullivan responded to the detective.

I'm glad Doug made sergeant. He's earned it.

"Did the photographer get here yet?" He got down on his haunches and then stood up, his knees creaking.

"No," said Sullivan pulling out his phone and glancing at it. "He said his ETA is 10 minutes."

"Great. Who found the body?" he asked, shaking out his legs.

"The dog," said a young, uniformed policewoman with a big smile, looking down at her notepad.

"The *dog?*" asked Williams.

Bizzy stepped forward. "Yes, Doug, my dog. Luigi."

"Okay. Coroner on the way?" He directed his question to the group of patrolmen.

"On her way," one of the officers called out.

Williams nodded. "Have you started interviewing everyone?" He motioned to all the houses.

"We have," said Officer Castelli. "We interviewed Elizabeth Devlin, owner of Saint Luigi Devlin, the dog who found the bones."

It sounded like a snicker from the officers standing to the side.

"Is this funny?" asked Williams.

A chorus of "No sir's" came from the group.

"Who else?" Williams sounded completely frustrated.

"Edith Tyne," said someone in a navy polo. "She actually owns this house. She's an airline attendant."

"Present!" Edy called out from the doorway of her house.

"Okay," said Williams. "Who else?"

The group seemed to be doing a lot more work now, or trying to look busy. Some were looking at and picking up different things in the sand. Occasionally someone would pick up something and put it in an evidence bag.

Bizzy turned to Doug. "Doug, just so you know, I'm doing some renovations, and most of the stuff in the sand is probably old."

A young man arrived with a small camera. Bizzy's face scrunched up. Edy came out of her house and moved closer to Bizzy. "Don't be so judgmental," she whispered. "He's probably just starting out his career."

"Where do you want me to start shooting?" asked the young man.

Williams turned to him and then pointed back to the body. "With the body?"

"That's a *body*?" asked the young photographer, glancing at the bones.

"Used to be," said Sullivan.

Bizzy and Edy looked on. Bizzy turned to Edy. "I can barely watch. He should shoot the wider scene first and then go in tight."

"Oh, stop," Edy said.

They heard footsteps behind them. Schaeffer loomed in the background but didn't come very close. His Hawaiian shirt was open even though it wasn't really hot, and his grey striped shorts hung down below his stomach.

"Looks like Schaeffer dressed for the occasion," said Edy.

Bizzy nonchalantly turned as if she were looking for Luigi. "He knows how to make a fashion statement. Black socks with sandals, very nice."

"It's what all the cool kids are wearing." Edy laughed a little too loud, and Williams turned to both women.

"Who's dead?" shouted Schaeffer.

Everyone stared at Schaeffer. Williams walked over to him. "Sir, we don't know yet."

"Oh, the body doesn't have a face?" Schaeffer asked.

"Ew," said Bizzy, "it's just bones. But human bones."

"How do you know they're human?" asked Schaeffer in his usual belligerent tone.

Williams now stood before all three of them. "Why don't you three go over there, and we'll come over and talk to you when we are done here?"

Schaeffer nodded but didn't move, and Edy seemed to be planted in place, too.

"Are we going to do what he asked?" Bizzy asked Edy.

"Nope," Edy answered, staring at Williams as she said it. "This is my property, and I'm going to watch what they do." Schaeffer stood there, too. "Hey, Bertie," said Edy, "you have to skedaddle."

"I want to know why there's human bones underneath your deck. Or where there used to be a deck," said Schaeffer.

"I don't know, Bertie, but I'm hoping to find out too," Edy said.

"Hey, what's going on here? Is this a party?" came the pleasant voice of another neighbor, Fred Long.

Two more people were coming up the boardwalk with a stretcher.

"Seems to me," said Schaeffer, "you may not need a stretcher, but maybe a shoebox or something." Schaeffer snorted after he said that, and Bizzy realized he was laughing. The snorting got a little louder.

"Okay!" Williams shouted. "Anyone who doesn't want to get arrested for interfering with a police investigation, get back!"

Bizzy walked to her door and stepped inside. The dog, who had been looking out the window, was excited to see her. Bizzy hadn't realized it, but he had been yelping to come out.

"Officer," said Edy, "I'm watching this. This is *my* house." And she stood watching from just inside her doorway.

He pointed to Fred Long and Schaeffer. "You two, stand over there."

"Hey," Fred smiled, "are you Dougie Williams?"

"*That's* Dougie Williams?" asked Schaeffer.

"Are you in Pullen Pointe now?" asked Fred. "You were somewhere else, weren't you?"

Williams nodded, "Yes, I was."

Bizzy opened her window so she could hear everything. "Of course he was somewhere else. He was in Cranberry."

"Oh," said Fred, "this must be a step up."

A few faint chuckles could be heard from the other police officers.

"*Is* Pullen Pointe a step up?" asked Bizzy through the open window. More chuckles. Williams ignored the question.

Lobsterman lumbered past Bizzy's house from the beach with a bucket of lobsters. He didn't stop to ask about the gathering of people. Just kept walking at his usual measured pace.

"Hey, Lobsterman, somebody's skeleton was buried under Bizzy and Edy's deck!" Schaeffer announced.

"Not my business," Lobsterman replied, keeping his head down. He continued to plod down the boardwalk with his catch, past the crowd of people and toward his house.

The kid shooting the forensic photos took several different angles. He tripped over rotted pieces of driftwood near the body. It was all Bizzy could do keep from giving advice. *Be careful! You're going to trash the crime scene.*

Luigi stood on his hind feet and leaned his forepaws on the windowsill. He looked from left to right, watching the police as they worked. Occasionally the puppy growled softly at the group of strangers intruding in his home territory.

THE FORENSIC DEPARTMENT finally arrived on the scene, and suddenly the area between the houses was awash in yellow tape. Bizzy recognized someone, but they were all suited up. "No crime scene contamination" was the name of the game when sifting through and collecting evidence.

The members of the team picked up different things and put them in bags, marking them, then putting them in a special box. Bizzy watched Doug go around and around the area. He then came back to her.

"You took photos?" asked Doug Williams.

"Yeah - kind of like a habit. When I used to do forensic photos, things would sometimes get messed up before I arrived at a crime scene. Didn't want that to happen this time around," Bizzy said. She put her head down. *Don't say it, Doug. Don't remind me of the time I messed up that case.*

"You'll give me copies, right?" He gave her a sideways

glance. Bizzy had worked with him at several police stations as their crime photographer. She had last seen Doug in Cranberry when he worked a case as a detective there.

"Why do you keep moving departments?" Bizzy asked. She gasped when she heard the words and realized they were not just in her head.

He paused a moment, surprised and amused at her question. "Money." He turned to her and smirked. "Prestige."

She chuckled softly. "I hope you get more money and prestige here than in Cranberry, but I doubt it."

Doug turned and watched the forensics team, sifting through sand. "Sorry about Dan. I forgot you guys lived here."

"Thanks," she said. "Me, too. But I'm moving forward." She waited a moment. "Sorry about Rita."

He smiled. "She didn't die."

"Divorce is no fun, either."

Doug Williams' face softened a little. Bizzy noticed his slightly receding hairline. *Cute. And he's got nice eyes,* using a term her mother had used all the time. People had "nice eyes," her mom would say when she couldn't think of anything else nice to say. Doug Williams had nice eyes *and* was cute. Bizzy noticed he had gained just a bit of weight, but she knew him. He would lose it fast.

"So, Bizzy," asked Doug, "tell me - what's going on here? Why'd you pick up the deck?"

Bizzy pointed to Howie and his boys standing at the corner of the property. "See those guys? Before they move forward with the major renovations on my house, they have to check the foundation. They had a structural engineer here and everything this morning. So, I'm paying them to stand there and watch." She shook her head.

A woman bent down to examine the remains, then stood up and removed her mask. Dr. Shirley Townsend, the medical examiner, was a curvy woman, 5'10" tall, in her late 40s with no-nonsense short-cropped hair - brown with a few silver streaks showing. Shirley said, "Hey, Biz", and walked over to Doug. "That body has been dead a long time."

"I figured as much, since it's just bones." Williams waited for laugh or a smile from Townsend. Nothing. "How long?" Doug asked.

"Hard to say for sure. Offhand I'd say over 15 years. But I'll have to run some tests." Shirley squatted down next to the remains. She continued, "It seems the guy was wearing a uniform."

"What kind of uniform?" Doug asked.

"Pullen Pointe jail guard, from the looks of it."

"The jail's been closed for over twenty years," said Bizzy.

"More like twenty-five," Edy called out.

"Anything else?" Doug asked the medical examiner.

"Part of the clothing had a name, so I'm guessing it's the name of the guard."

"What's the name?"

"Most of it is deteriorated. The only letters I can make out are "ian", all lower case."

Doug motioned to the remains. "Could that guy have been there for over twenty-five years?"

Townsend shrugged, "Sure, why not?"

"Sand erosion, storms--"

Dr. Townsend walked to where she could see the beach. She said, "There's a beach wall out front. And," pointing to the skeleton, "this area seems pretty protected."

They started to walk away. "When do you think you're going to have some answers here?" Doug asked.

Bizzy strained to hear the answer, but they were further away now, and she wasn't able to catch it.

Rubber bicycle tires squealed against the wooden boardwalk. Then a suitcase hit the ground with a thump. Howie and the guys turned and started laughing. Jacko was walking a bicycle up the boardwalk, attempting to balance a suitcase and other bags, without much success. He saw Bizzy and the crowd of people assembled.

"What's going on, Biz? A party for me? Aw - you shouldn't have."

Jacko saw Doug Williams beside Bizzy. With a puzzled look, he asked, "Why is Dougie here?"

"Come on up," Bizzy said.

He passed a group of neighbors, including Edy, and noticed their dour faces. "Wow, what happened? Did someone die?" His suitcase crashed to the ground again.

"St. Luigi dug up some bones," Bizzy said.

Jacko looked around. "All these people are here because a dog dug up some bones? Are they going to put him in doggy jail?" Jacko chuckled at his own joke after he had said it. Bizzy remained stone-faced.

"Um, they were *human* bones," said Bizzy.

"So you're saying he's in the dog house." Jacko laughed again. He stopped abruptly when he saw Bizzy's stoic face.

"Very funny. You can take your stuff in the house. You will have the bedroom upstairs on the right."

CHAPTER SIX

B izzy looked toward the cordoned-off area and Howie standing there. Then she faced Doug with a question in her eyes.

Doug said, "I don't know how long we're going to need the crime scene to stay intact."

"So what do I tell my contractor?"

Doug shrugged.

"Shrugging is not an answer," said Bizzy.

Doug looked at Shirley Townsend, who said, "Well, you're not going to like this, but this body is old. So it's going to take some time. We've got to make sure we don't lose anything. We will probably be sifting through the sand around it. The best I can do is a couple of days."

Bizzy groaned. "Okay. I have to tell the contractor."

"How long before you can identify it?" Doug asked the M.E.

"Don't know. We will probably be going by dental records," Townsend said. "But if we locate the jail employee records, we might be able to establish the identity that way."

"Any idea how he was killed?" Doug asked, scrawling away in his notebook.

"Right now my best guess is a blow to the skull, but I can't say for sure," said the M.E. "The skull could have been damaged some other way after death."

Edy stood back from Doug, Bizzy, and the medical examiner, but she was listening to every word. The medical examiner began to carefully put evidence into bags.

Edy stepped outside her door. "I don't know why a jail guard would be on my...," Edy started to breathe heavily, and her voice wavered, "On my, my property." Edy started to cry, and Bizzy walked over and wrapped an arm around her.

"I barely remember the jail," Bizzy said as she held her crying friend. "I never knew anyone who even worked there. Did you?" Bizzy noticed that Edy's face was down and she was moving the sand around her feet with her toes.

She nodded. "Yes." She continued, "Bizzy, you actually know two people who worked at the jail," said Edy. She motioned behind them to the small crowd that had formed.

Bizzy turned to look. "Who?"

"Edy pointed her finger. Fred Long and Bertie Schaeffer."

"Oh yeah," Bizzy said. "I knew that."

Doug looked at Fred. "Is that so, Mr. Long?" he asked.

"Yeah, I worked there for over 25 years."

Long pointed to Schaeffer, "He did, too."

Schaeffer said nothing, but Bizzy noticed that he glared at Long for several seconds.

Why the look, Schaeffer?

"A lot of guards lived here back in the day," Long said, glancing at Edy."

Doug looked up at the two women. "Anybody else

around here have anything to do with the jail?"

"A lot of people from here, East Boston, and Revere used to work there." Edy said. "Easy commute."

Bizzy did remember a guy who had worked at the jail, but moved when he realized that he'd have to go through Boston every day to get to work.

"I..." Edy stammered a little. "I used to rent a room to someone who worked at the jail. Tony. Tony Giancarlo."

Bizzy looked at Edy, wide-eyed. "You never told me that!"

"Believe me, girl, it was a long time ago. Way before your time at the Pointe," Edy said. A sadness came over her face. "And one day he just up and left."

They both heard some coughing and turned to see Long going into a coughing spell.

Doug did some scrawling on his notepad. Bizzy craned her head to get a better look at the notes. But Doug did a quarter turn with his body, so she couldn't see his notes. "So, Ms. Tyne, what can you tell me about this Tony Giancarlo fellow?"

"He was a guard," Edy said. "He rented a room from me, and well, I needed the money. I had a three-year old to feed, and so, I rented him a room."

"Which room?" asked Bizzy, scanning her brain to visualize the rooms in Edy's house. *That house is so small.*

"It's part of the kitchen now. The room had a single bed and a small dresser, and he rented it for $100 a month. That money was food for the month for me and Jay." She glanced over to Bizzy.

"What happened to him?" asked Doug.

Edy shook her head, "Don't know. He just left one day. Don't know where he went."

"That's odd," said Doug, "that he'd just up and leave."

"It *was* odd, and he didn't take his belongings. He didn't have much, but when he didn't come back after a month, I called his family. They didn't show any interest, so that was that."

Bizzy noticed a strange tone in Edy's voice. *What's going on?*

"I missed the money, but I eventually got the job with the airline, and now I do just fine," said Edy. She smiled after she said that. Bizzy knew it was her fake smile. *Oh, Edith Tyne, you have some questions coming your way when I get you alone.*

Doug handed Edy a card. "If you think of anything, Edith - a break-out, an escape, anything from around that time - please let me know."

"Detective, it wasn't a high security prison. It was a county jail," Edy said, tapping the card on her hand.

Bizzy said nothing to her friend, but her mind raced. *You had a tenant?*

～

AS SOON AS Doug was out of earshot, Bizzy asked Edy, "So what happened to him?"

Edy shrugged, "I told you. I don't know, he just left."

Bizzy stared at her friend. "He just left? Was it when the jail closed?"

"He left 'bout a year before the jail closed." Edy glanced away. "He came home one day, and he seemed out of sorts. Then he left for work for the third shift. At least that's what I thought. And he was gone. Didn't say good-bye and didn't take any of his things. Just himself."

They watched as the forensics team carefully scooped up more of the sand and bones and sifted it in a square sifter. The bones they found were put in a special container. Two women carefully marked and carried everything away from the scene.

"How long was he your..." Bizzy realized she didn't quite know the term.

"My boarder. My tenant. We didn't make a big deal of the terms. It was a tenant-at-will situation." Edy turned away from Bizzy.

"I can't get over that he just left," Bizzy mused.

"Can we just not talk about it?" There was more than a hint of frustration in Edy's voice.

Bizzy stepped back. "Ohhh...kay."

Edy walked to her door and went into the house. Bizzy just watched as she went in. She felt a touch on her shoulder and spun around. Jacko stood there with a backpack and another suitcase. Bizzy bumped into the suitcase, and it fell over.

"Oh, you have more stuff?" *He's got more stuff than I do!*

"So whose bones did they find?" asked Jacko.

"It looks like it could have been a jail guard."

"What jail?"

Bizzy pointed to Pullen Pointe Park, at the tip of the peninsula. "Over there."

"There's a *jail* there?"

Bizzy said, "There was, years ago. County jail. It was an old, decrepit place. It had been built in the 1800s as an Ellis Island-type place for new immigrants, and then it became a jail. It also served as a military lookout place during World War II. Apparently they decided to turn it into a park, so they moved the prisoners and tore down the jail. Some of those small buildings still around the park are from that time. But now it's just a park. And a place where people fish."

Bizzy and Jacko looked over the park, lush and green. People walked the asphalt trail put in after the jail was dismantled. It had large rocks around the edge. A lone fisherman cast his pole into the water off one of the rocks.

After the police and the rest of the crowd finally left, Bizzy went over, knocked on Edy's door, and walked in. "Hey, Edy!" she called out to her friend.

Edy was sitting on her couch, her head in her hands. "It's him." Edy said, without looking up.

"Who?" Bizzy asked.

"It's Tony."

"The guard you rented to? How can you be so sure?"

"Bizzy, Tony disappeared suddenly, without any notice."

"It might not be him. He could have left town. That's what you thought 'til today, isn't it?"

"Yes, until today," Edy answered. There was a deep sadness in her eyes.

"Come to think of it," Bizzy said, "the medical examiner did say the name on the uniform had and 'i-a-n' on it. That fits 'Giancarlo.' So that part actually matches."

"It's him. I can feel it in my bones."

"You can't be sure, Edy."

"It's him. And what's more, the police are going to think that *I* killed him."

"No way!" Bizzy said, trying to reassure her friend.

"I'm telling you they will. Think about it. He was *my* tenant who disappeared suddenly. And his body turns up practically on my doorstep."

"Edy, don't worry. Doug is a good detective, and even if those end up being Tony's remains, Doug will look at the evidence and conclude that you are innocent."

"Mark my words, Bizzy Devlin. They will think I did it."

CHAPTER SEVEN

The next morning Jacko and Bizzy took Luigi out for a walk on the beach.

Bizzy and Jacko threw the ball along the sand as they walked. The puppy chased it with gusto and brought it back to them. Bizzy held out a treat and gave the command, "Drop the ball." Luigi dropped the ball on the ground in front of Bizzy. "Now sit." He obeyed, and she gave him a treat.

"Okay little guy, go get the ball!" And she threw the ball again. For such a young pup, Luigi was very fast.

But other times Luigi brought the ball right to Jacko. The puppy jumped up on him, begging him to wrestle the ball from his mouth and throw it. Jacko happily obliged and played the game that Luigi was teaching him. "Hey, Lou, you sure are playful today!"

This went on until Luigi's tongue was hanging out of his mouth, and his fetching slowed to a trot. "I think you've had enough running for now," Jacko said to the worn-out canine.

As they neared the house, Bizzy heard the sound of sobbing coming from Edy's place.

"Jacko, take the dog, please." She handed him the leash as she ran towards Edy's house.

She reached the screen door and could see Edy at her kitchen table, head in hands. "No, no, no!" Bizzy swung open the door and ran in. She stopped short when she saw Officer Bertrand standing near the kitchen sink.

Bizzy turned to him. "What's wrong? Is Jay okay?"

Edy nodded. "Jay is fine."

"We identified the body," said Bertrand.

"Okay," Bizzy said, afraid to ask. "Who is it?"

"It's someone I know - or *knew*," Edy blubbered her words.

Bizzy heard a rustling behind the door. She hadn't noticed Doug standing there. He looked down at his notebook, "It's Anthony Giancarlo."

With the sound of the name, Edy cried harder.

"I'm so sorry," Bizzy said to Edy, who was now heaving with sobs.

Bizzy then twisted around toward Doug. "So how'd he end up here?" Bizzy asked. In the silent pause, Edy tried to catch her breath. Bizzy pulled a chair up next to her friend's. She glanced around the room for a box of tissues and handed some to Edy.

Bizzy saw a man in the shadows she didn't recognize. Doug introduced him. "Bizzy, this is Detective Tim Martin. He's been on the force for two years."

"Hi, Tim," Bizzy said, and she patted her friend's back. "It's okay, Edy. It's okay."

"He lived here..." Edy drifted before she began crying again.

"Okay," Bizzy said.

Jacko came to the door and looked in through the screen. Bizzy saw him and gave a little wave.

Martin saw him, too. "Who's that?"

"Jacko. Giacomo Rossi, I call him Jacko," Bizzy said.

"Come in, Giacomo," Edy said. He opened the door a little and entered the room, which left Luigi peering in. "You can let the little guy in, too. He doesn't like being separated from his mama."

"Edy, we'd really like to ask you a few questions about Anthony Giancarlo," Doug said.

"I want my friends to stay," said Edy.

Detective Martin started questioning Edy, and she explained what she'd told Bizzy the day before.

Doug stepped forward from behind the door. "How well did you know Mr. Giancarlo?"

As Edy inhaled deeply, her sobbing subsided. "I knew him well. We were friends. Close friends."

"Was there anything-?"

"How was he murdered?" Bizzy asked Doug, interrupting.

"Please, ma'am," Tim started, speaking to Bizzy.

Bizzy cut him off. "Don't call me ma'am. I hate being referred to that way."

Tim glared at her.

"Okay, Bizzy. Relax," Doug said a bit defensively, but he offered her a smile.

Dougie does not like Tim Martin. "Sorry. Tim, you can call me Bizzy, or Ms. Devlin, or some combo, but not ma'am."

Edy smiled at this.

At this point Doug stepped in. "So, Edy," he asked, "what do you remember about the last time you saw Tony?"

"I remember thinking," her voice soft was soft, almost a whisper, "'why is he working the third shift so much?'"

"Okay," Doug continued, "why would that strike you as odd? Didn't he have to alternate shifts?"

"He had enough seniority that he usually worked first or second shift. He liked the second shift best. It wasn't 'til the last month or two that he started working the third shift more and more. And he started taking on some doubles."

"Did he give a reason for the change?" Bizzy asked.

Tim Martin glared at Bizzy and snapped his notebook shut.

"Tony didn't talk about his work very much with me," Edy said.

Bizzy kept her eyes fixed on Doug. She knew she should probably keep her eye on Tim, who looked like a spanking new detective in his new detective suit, with his new detective notebook. She felt very protective of her friend.

"Bizzy, I'm going to ask the questions, okay?" Doug said it in a very calm tone, even though his detective partner sighed.

"Okay. Just asking some obvious questions," Bizzy replied.

"Edy, do you remember him talking about anything that might have led to his death?"

"Nothing that I can think of."

Detective Martin rolled his eyes and huffed at Edy.

"You know, Tim," said Doug, "I'd like to talk to Edy by myself for a sec." He tossed the younger detective the car keys. "Could you go down and wait for me at the car?"

Detective Martin glared at Doug. He walked toward the door. Bizzy heard Tim say under his breath, "This is not proper procedure." Detective Young And Brash slammed the door on his way out.

Luigi went over to Edy and wrapped her feet with his

body. He licked her ankle, and Edy let out a little laugh. "Little boy, I'm ticklish."

"So, you and Anthony..." Doug began a question.

Edy cut him off. "He liked to be called Tony."

"Right. So you and Tony were good friends. Was there anything more to the relationship?"

Edy reached down and patted Luigi on the head. The room fell silent.

"Yes. We were actually, at one point, together."

Whoa! Bizzy raised her eyebrows. *Who is this person sitting next to me?*

"At first we were landlady and tenant. And then friends. And then, more than friends."

All these years Edy had told Bizzy that she was fine just being by herself. She now realized that her friend kept a heart-wrenching secret. *Why couldn't she tell me?*

Bizzy felt for Edy. *Come on Dougie, be gentle with my friend.*

"So," Doug continued, "there were no fights or anything?"

"Never," Edy snapped. "I mean, we had our moments. We were young, and Tony always said being Italian meant being loud. And back then, I could hold my own."

Hold my own? Edy?

Bizzy watched as her friend twirled her fingers and massaged her hands on her lap. Luigi sat up and placed his head on her lap for easy petting. She looked at him, stroking the hair out of his eyes.

"Can you tell me if anything was going on at the jail?" Doug's voice was gentle.

"I already told you, Tony didn't talk to me about his work at the jail."

"But everything was fine between the two of you?"

Now there were just tears. More tears on already drenched cheeks. She nodded.

"What did you do with his belongings?"

"I gathered what little he had in a couple of boxes. Clothes and some personal items. I contacted his family, but they didn't want it. So I put the boxes in the attic, in case he came back looking for his things."

Edy didn't raise her head. She stared at the floor or Luigi, who gazed at her with big puppy eyes.

"We'll want to take a look at those belongings. If you can get them from the attic, I will send an officer over to pick them up." Doug took a card out of his jacket pocket. "If you remember anything, Edy, call me, please."

She nodded.

Doug walked out the door.

As the big droplets began to fall onto Edy's hands, Luigi licked up her tears. In one swift motion, he got up on his hind legs and put his paws on her arms and her shoulders. Her face was crestfallen, and Luigi licked the tears on her cheeks, trying to catch them as they fell from her eyes. Edy reached out and put her arms around the dog. Bizzy went over and sat next to her friend, also hugging her.

"It'll be all right Edy. Luigi knows it." The dog kept his eyes on Edy.

Edy turned to her and shook her head. "It's *not* all right. He was the love of my life. I thought he left me. But he's been buried here outside my house this whole time."

"I wonder who-" Bizzy started to say.

"They think it was *me*, Bizzy. All those questions they're asking - They think it was me. They're going to charge me with murder."

Edy pulled the dog in closer.

"I won't let that happen," Bizzy assured her friend. "I'll

investigate this myself before I let anyone accuse you of murder."

~

BIZZY AND JACKO left Edy's house, and Jacko started preparing lunch.

Bizzy heard her phone ping. "Mom."

She looked at him. "Do I have twenty minutes before lunch is ready?"

He nodded and smiled. She clicked the 'accept call' button.

"Can you turn the phone around so I can see my cute grand-puppy?" Diana asked. Bizzy pressed the screen on her phone and aimed it toward Luigi sleeping in his bed. "Is he tired, Bizzy? Sick?"

"He's been running on the beach, is all."

"Hello, Biz." She heard a low gravelly voice join the conversation on the other end of the line.

"Hey, Daddy."

"Stand up straight, Quint. You heard what the doctor said about your posture," said the off-screen voice of Diana.

"He just said to do some exercises," said Quint. Both of them were in the picture now. Well, at least half of each was.

"I can't see either of you," said Bizzy. "Or rather, I can see the top of your head, Mom, and the side of Dad's face, mainly his ear."

"There's the sweet puppy," Diana cooed. "When are you coming down, so I can meet him?"

"You are welcome to come up here." Bizzy rolled her eyes at Jacko.

"I know, I know," said Diana. "I'd have to fly, because your father doesn't want to make that drive anymore."

"I don't want to drive, because you do nothing but hiss and tell me to watch out," said Quint, who was now slightly more in the frame than Diana. Only a small swish of her reddish hair, with some tinges of gray, was in the video frame.

"Well, Mom and Dad, you could fly. Sean's job gives you free flights." Bizzy's brother, Sean, worked for a major airline.

"Oh, Bizzy, I'm not crazy about flying," Diana whined.

"I'll come up, Bizzy!" Quint laughed. "That way your mom can miss me."

"Quint, I wouldn't miss you." Diana laughed.

Out of the corner of her eye, Bizzy saw Jacko miming that lunch was ready. He pointed to the pot, and then pretended to be putting food into his mouth. She nodded. The dog moved toward Jacko as he was miming. Bizzy kept following the dog with the phone. The screen showed Luigi at Jacko's feet.

"Who's that?" Diana asked.

"That's Jacko," Bizzy said, switching the screen back to her face.

"Who is Jacko?" Quint asked sternly.

"You know Jacko, Dad. He's been here before when you've called. He's my assistant, and he's been taking care of the studio."

Both parents murmured at the same time.

"He and I have been working together now for a couple of years. He's really been running the show for the last several months as I've..." She looked over at Jacko. "As I've been getting back on my feet."

"Oh, okay," said Diana. "I think I remember him."

"Hi, Mr. & Mrs. Devlin," Jacko said in a sing-songy tone.

"Call me Diana," said Diana.

"Call me Mr. Devlin," said Quint.

Bizzy laughed. "Well, okay, introductions are over. We're - I'm going to eat now." The "we're" sounded odd to Bizzy.

"Okay, bye, Bizzy," they said in unison.

"Wow, you guys must have practiced!" laughed Bizzy. "Love you both. And Luigi does, too."

"How do I turn this off?" asked Diana, as Bizzy pressed the button.

Bizzy went over to the counter. "Smells good."

"I thought your mom might remember me," said Jacko.

"Yeah, she probably does. You were out of context for her right now," Bizzy replied as she picked up a piece of garlic bread and took a big bite. "That is a *lot* of garlic."

"That's bad?"

"No, absolutely delicious."

He put plates of pasta on the table. "Mangia."

"Don't mind if I do."

Remember, we need to spend the afternoon at the studio getting ready for the pet photoshoot," Bizzy said.

"I have a bunch of YouTube videos we can watch to prepare," Jacko replied with a smile.

CHAPTER EIGHT

The next morning Jacko had a pot of coffee brewing for Bizzy. He was sipping on a small cup of espresso. "Luigi is all peed and pooped, and he's eaten his breakfast," Jacko reported. "Would you like a bagel or eggs or something?"

Thanks, Jacko. I'd love one of those 'everything' bagels."

"Toasted?"

"Absolutely, with lots of cream cheese and some extra 'everything bagel' topping. I'm going to stop over next door for a minute to check on Edy."

"Sounds good. It will be ready when you get back."

Bizzy went next door, knocked, and stuck her head inside the door. "Good morning, sunshine. Just wanted to see how you're doing today."

"Thanks, Biz. I'm hanging in there. Trying to stay busy. As a matter of fact, just today I just came across a picture of Tony that was in an old book of mine. I didn't even remember that I still had that picture."

Tony had dark hair, a big warm smile that seemed to be a natural part of him, and a Roman nose. "He was a good looking guy." Bizzy took a quick picture of the photo with her phone.

"Yes he was. Not in the GQ sort of way. Just down-to-earth handsome."

"Glad to see you are doing better than yesterday. Let me know if you need anything."

"Maybe I will borrow your ladder a little later to get those boxes of stuff out of the attic."

"Of course. I can ask Jacko to lend a hand getting them down. Right now he has breakfast waiting for me."

Edy raised one eyebrow and looked at Bizzy with a knowing smile, but didn't say a word. She didn't have to.

"Yes, Edy, Jacko's a sweet guy and a good friend. But we are not 'a thing'. I am not thinking about that at all."

"Of course you're not."

～

BIZZY WALKED BACK to the house, and Luigi jumped up on her. "I'm glad you are excited to see me, Lou. I've been away nearly three whole minutes!"

Jacko laughed. "That little guy loves his mommy, for sure. And your breakfast is ready, Biz."

Bizzy made herself a coffee with cappuccino. She sank her teeth into the bagel that Jacko prepared. "Thanks, Jacko. This is delicious."

"My pleasure. The simple things of life." Jacko finished off the last of his own breakfast. "So what's the order of business for today?"

"Jacko, I want to go through these crime scene photos with a second set of eyes." Bizzy opened her laptop and pulled up the photos she had taken of the crime scene.

"Sure. As long as I don't get locked up if they throw you in jail for meddling in police affairs."

Bizzy rolled her eyes. "Ok, brave guy. I promise I won't rat you out and take you down with me. But just to put you at ease, we aren't *interfering* in a police investigation. We are *helping*."

"Good point - even if Dougie doesn't typically want our help." Jacko pulled up a chair while Bizzy brought the first of the photos to the large screen.

"Keep an eye open for anything unusual, or that might be helpful in clearing Edy," Bizzy instructed.

"Got it."

When she came to a shot of Tony's uniform and pocket, with a plastic lighter hanging partially out of it, Bizzy paused.

"Can you zoom in more on that lighter?" Jacko asked.

"There's some writing on the lighter," Bizzy said. "It's faded, but it looks like *Terminal M*. That name sounds familiar."

"*Terminal M* is a restaurant in East Boston," Jacko replied. "The M stands for Montini, the last name of the owner. Its claim to fame is that decades ago a small one-engine plane crashed into the roof on a foggy night while trying to land at the airport."

"Whoa!" said Bizzy. "I bet that gave all the clients indigestion."

Jacko chuckled. "Very funny. The plane crashed after hours. Miraculously, not even the pilot was hurt. Joey Montini, the owner of the restaurant, decided to leave the plane right there, stuck in the roof. He figured it would give some character to the place. But believe me, that place has plenty of character even without the plane."

"Oh, I know that place," Bizzy said. "I've passed it once

or twice, but I've never been inside. After we finish going through these photos, let's go have lunch there. Maybe we can dig up some helpful information about Tony."

∼

AS THEY PULLED up to the restaurant, Bizzy saw the little Piper Cub sticking out of the roof next to the *Terminal M* sign. There was a sign inside the entrance that said, "Seat yourself. If nobody attends you, just lasso one of the waiters." Jacko grabbed two menus and showed Bizzy to a small booth.

"Hey, Giacomo," a waiter called out with a mischievous grin as he carried a delicious-smelling meatball sub to a client at another table. "This little lady is even prettier than the one you brought in last week!"

"Don't be spreading rumors about me, Salvatore," Jacko called back, playing the part. "This little lady is my boss."

"Well then, I will behave myself," Sal said. He paused. "A little."

"Does everyone know everyone here?" Bizzy asked.

"Almost," Jacko answered. "Once you've been in here two or three times, you can expect to be called by your first name. Just that kind of place."

After ordering a "BLT without the T" from Sal, Bizzy noticed a wall of photos and asked Jacko about them. "These are pictures of clients over the years. Lots of the pictures were taken here, and the ones with the bumper stickers that say 'I love *Terminal M*' were taken by loyal clients traveling around the world."

While they waited for their order, Bizzy and Jacko looked over the photo wall. From behind them, a low, gravelly voice said, "Hey, Giacomo, good to see you. So who's your friend?"

They turned around to see the 81-year old owner of the restaurant, Joey Montini. He was nearly bald but had clear blue eyes and was smiling with a perfect set of dentures. He had been a Marine and always stood with a ramrod straight back. Joey personally knew all the regular patrons of *Terminal M* over the last several decades and made it a point to get to know the new ones.

"Biz, this is Joey Montini, the owner of *Terminal M*. Joey, this is my friend and boss-lady, Bizzy Devlin. Her photography studio is over in Pullen Pointe."

"A photographer? Do you like our photo wall? It started out as just a bulletin board. And when we kept on adding more and more photos, I got the idea to use a whole wall for clients' photos. Most of the photos are not professional looking or anything. But I figured people would feel a little more at home seeing their pictures on our wall."

"I love the photo wall, Mr. Montini. And photos don't necessarily need to be professionally done to make people feel welcome at the place."

Joey beamed with pride. "Please, call me Joey. All my friends call me Joey. And any friend of Giacomo's is a friend of mine."

"Then Joey it is." Bizzy noticed a large photo of a group of people. Joey Montini was standing behind the group, wrapping his arms around as many as he could reach. She pointed to the photo. "Can you tell me about this one?"

"That picture is the last Christmas party for the staff of the Pullen Pointe Jail before they closed down the jail. And that's me in back - 25 years younger, and with a full head of hair."

Something in the photo caught Bizzy's eye. "These two faces look familiar," she said.

"That's Fred Long and Bertie Schaeffer," Joey said.

"Wow! I hardly recognized them. They look so young here!" Bizzy replied. "Oh, and this looks like Tony Giancarlo."

"Yeah, that's him," Joey said. "I heard about his body turning up recently. That's a shame. Tony was a nice guy."

"And who is this pretty blonde lady next to Tony?" Bizzy asked.

"That's Angela. Her married name at that time might have been Biggio. Angela went through a few husbands. She was a popular girl, if you know what I mean." Wink, wink.

"Were she and Tony especially friendly?"

"Nah." Joey paused. "Well, not that I know of. But with Angela, you didn't always know."

"And where is Angela now?" Jacko asked the owner.

"Last I heard she was still living somewhere in East Boston. But I haven't seen her at our fine establishment in a while."

Bizzy and Jacko thanked Joey, finished their lunch, and headed home.

"We have to go find this Angela woman," Bizzy said.

"Why did I know you were going to say that?"

WHEN BIZZY and Jacko got home, Edy was on the top of the three steps leading to her door, which she called "the stoop." That was Edy's way of signaling that she was in a mood to chat. A big pile of sand was next to the spot where Luigi had found the bones, and there were little piles of sand everywhere. Bizzy sat on the bottom step, her feet on the sand. Edy stared at the mounds around them. She brought her usual cup of black coffee up to her lips. She used the same cup all day, and if possible, it was the same cup as the day before.

"Want some cold coffee?" asked Edy.

"You mean iced coffee?" Bizzy asked.

"No, I mean cold coffee that has been in the pot all day and tastes pretty much like tar," said Edy. She turned toward Bizzy and stretched out her arm with the cup.

"Edy, I'm thinking that stuff does really bad things to your body." Bizzy smiled. A gust of wind came up and ripped a strip of the yellow tape from where it had been attached to Bizzy's house. It slowly drifted to the ground.

"This is really going to slow your renovation," Edy said.

Bizzy realized Edy was trying to avoid bringing up the subject of Tony. "Probably. I heard Howie talking to his crew about another house on Neptune Street they were going to start working on in the meantime." Bizzy turned to her friend, who stared out into the distance. Her index finger tapped the cup she clung to.

"Edy, what's going on inside that head of yours?" Bizzy wanted to find out more about Edy's former tenant but didn't want to upset her more.

"Nothing. Nothing," she said, turning to Bizzy.

"Not buying it, Edy. You might as well open up to me."

She put her cup down and placed both hands on her face. "Oh, Bizzy," she said, shaking her head, "all these years I have lived believing Tony up and left with no explanation, not even a goodbye. We really had something together. Or at least I thought we did..." A tear formed in her eye and started to run down her cheek.

"I'm so sorry, Edy," Bizzy said. She moved up to Edy's step and put her arm around her friend. "So sorry."

"But now I come to find out he was murdered and buried practically at my doorstep all this time." Edy's tears began to flow freely now, and she laid her head on Bizzy's shoulder and sobbed.

Bizzy just held Edy in her arms, pulled her close, and let her cry, until eventually the sobbing subsided.

Edy lifted her head and looked at Bizzy. "You know what it's like to lose someone you love dearly?" she asked.

Bizzy was silent for a moment, and a tear came to her eye. "I do, Edy." The two friends just sat for a while in silence.

"Thanks for understanding, Biz - for being a good friend and a shoulder to lean on. I thought I had put the whole thing behind me years ago. But yesterday just ripped the bandage off the wound, and it's terribly fresh and painful."

"That must have been so hard for you back then. What happened when he didn't come home?"

"Well, I called up to the jail, and they said he hadn't gone there, either. He just stopped going to work."

"Did you rent out the room again?"

Edy replied, "I tried for a while, but not that hard. To tell you the truth, I didn't really want another person in there. I guess some part of me held out hope that Tony would come back."

There was that rare silence between the two friends.

Edy took another swig of coffee, and then stared into the cup. "Gone."

"Gone?" Bizzy asked.

"The coffee," Edy breathed in the brisk fall air. "Besides, everybody was saying I wouldn't get any more renters. Since with the jail closing soon, nobody would want to rent a place around here. But there always seem to be airline people needing a place. So I just wasn't thinking. The truth is, I really didn't *want* anyone else here."

"I don't blame you." She looked straight at her friend. "Edy, are you, are you gonna be okay?"

"I guess. It just brings up bad memories. I thought there was a real possibility that Tony and I would be together for a lifetime. I was 28 at the time, and he was a good-looking guy from East Boston, and I just thought we'd get together."

"How did Tony and Jay get along?" Bizzy asked.

Edy looked at Bizzy and smiled. "Oh, Tony liked Jay a lot. He was actually kind of a good father figure. As you know, Jay never had that with his dad. So Tony did a good job of filling in. He played ball with him and even talked about being his baseball coach when Jay was old enough. Even at such a young age, Jay started getting attached to him. So I was brokenhearted for Jay, too, that he left without so much as a note."

"That must have been so hard for you both." Bizzy removed a strand of police tape that blew across her foot.

"That's when I just kind of gave up on I-don't-know-what. Tony wasn't perfect. He had had some issues in the past. But he was trying to get a brand new start. And I loved that about him." She leaned back against the house and breathed a sigh.

"What issues?"

"Tony liked his wine, and at one time had been too attached to his Italian 'grappa.' But that was before I knew him - old demons that he had left behind. I never saw him drink. And he was kind. He was good to me and to Jay. Oh, well. I don't know what to say." She sighed.

Bizzy stood up and looked at Edy. "You know, Doug will

be sending someone for the boxes of Tony's stuff. Maybe we could get those down? What do you think would be there?"

"I don't remember really. But I'm not up to that today."

"We don't need to do it now. I can't believe you kept his stuff."

"Why? It's mostly just old clothes. But it's all I have of him. I just thought he'd come back..."

"You really loved this guy, didn't you?"

"Yes, yes I did. And for a time I thought he might come back to me and Jay." Tears welled up in her eyes again. She just stood there.

Bizzy said, "Edy, the jail had been closed for a long time when Dan and I got together. But you say Fred Long and Schaeffer worked at the jail, too."

"Yes, they did. I thought one of them would have known what happened to Tony, Fred especially. He and Tony were kind of close."

"Fred didn't know what happened to him?"

Edy shook her head, "No, and I think he was angry with Tony for having left me. Fred was very supportive of me when Tony disappeared. Actually, Schaeffer was, too."

"I can believe Fred would be supportive. Schaeffer, not so much."

"Biz, Schaeffer was a nicer man before Jeannie got sick and then passed away."

"I keep forgetting that."

"It was Fred who gave me the hostas." Edy laughed. "He wasn't real happy that little LuLu destroyed them. But hey, I didn't ask him to plant them in the first place."

Jacko knocked and popped his head in the door. "Hey there, ladies. How are you doing?" Luigi came in between Jacko's legs and went to Edy, who stroked his head and scratched gently behind his ears. Luigi nuzzled Edy and licked her hands.

"To tell you the truth, not great, Giacomo. But as well as can be expected under the circumstances," Edy replied. "Thanks for asking."

"Jacko, can you grab the ladder behind the house and help Edy get the boxes of Tony's stuff out of the attic?" Bizzy asked.

"Sure. Be back in a sec."

Less than a minute later, Jacko came back with a six-foot stepladder and put it under the old plywood panel that served as the door to Edy's attic. Jacko pushed the makeshift door up and slid it aside into the attic.

Edy handed Jacko a flashlight. "It's just a couple of plain brown boxes the back corner of the attic marked 'Tony's belongings.'"

Jacko spotted the boxes, reached in, handed them to Edy and Bizzy below, and closed the attic door.

"Just leave them for now," Edy said. "I'll go through them a little later."

"Let us know if you need anything, Edy. We have a shoot at the studio," Bizzy said. And she and Jacko left Edy to her thoughts.

CHAPTER NINE

That evening, Bizzy made Edy a cup of hot herbal tea. Edy didn't really want it, but Bizzy had to do something. She made sure her friend was in bed, then left with Luigi. When Bizzy walked in her door, Luigi headed upstairs to Jacko. She heard the two of them romping up in the spare bedroom where Jacko was now staying. *I'm glad those two get along so well.*

A minute later they came down the stairs, and Luigi immediately began jumping on Bizzy.

"Down boy, down." Bizzy went into the kitchen and turned her electric kettle on. She stood over the sink for a minute, looking at her reflection in the window.

"Are you okay?" Jacko asked.

"Yeah, I guess."

"This is so awful. It sounds like she was really in love with Tony."

"She's never mentioned him. Not once, Jacko. Don't you find that strange? I mean, we've been friends for a really long time."

"It sounds like it was awful for her."

"I told her everything."

Jacko went over to the cabinet with the cups and pulled down two. "Is there enough water for two cups?"

Bizzy nodded, then took a long deep breath. "She is one of the best friends I have in the world. She," Bizzy turned to Jacko, "and you got me through this past year."

Jacko put tea bags in the cups.

"She's right, Jacko. The police are going to think she did it."

"Because the body was found on her property?"

"That, and she was his girlfriend. And-"

"They would have to have more evidence than that, right?"

"Yes, but it could be really tough on her. When there is a murder, it's pretty common that the spouse or lover did it."

The kettle started to beep and Jacko put up a hand. "I'll get it. Lemon and honey?"

Bizzy nodded. "How did the body get there? Dang, if I wasn't doing all this renovation, it never would have been found."

"Yeah, but it still would have been there."

Jacko, you have a weird way of hitting the nail on the head.

"You're right. So what happened?"

Jacko handed Bizzy the cup of tea. She looked at him. "I just can't figure out when the body was put there."

Jacko shook his head.

"Here's the thing: Ten years ago Dan and Jay took up all the old boards and then put the new deck down. The body would have shown up then, right?"

Jacko nodded and took a sip of his tea.

"So why didn't we find it then?" Bizzy glanced in the direction of where the body was found.

"It should have been found then," Jacko said.

"Maybe the machine helped get it loose or something. How long would Tony have been dead? Almost 25 years? I think Edy was 30. Jay was three or four. So what really happened?"

"Is there a chance the body was there when Dan and Jay did the deck, but they didn't notice? That they didn't dig that deep?" Jacko said.

Bizzy took a small sip of the tea and set the cup down. "There's no way that there was a body there, because the old boards had been there for a lot of years. At least thirty years before Dan and Jay did the new deck. Maybe more."

"Well, that answers that." Jacko sipped his tea.

THE NEXT DAY Bizzy eased into the parking spot she found fairly close to the Pullen Pointe Police Station. It had, at one time, been the post office and still had "U.S. Post Office" inscribed in cement over the door.

She hadn't been in the police station for a while. In the past it had been to drop off photos or talk about the photos she took of crime scenes.

Feel like I haven't been in here in a hundred years.

The counter area was still the same, but now a young blonde woman in a uniform sat in a tall chair behind the counter. She was on the phone. She smiled at Bizzy and lifted her index finger up to indicate she would be a minute. Bizzy stood there looking at all the fine carvings that used to be decor for the post office.

"Can I help you?" the policewoman asked as she hung up the phone.

"Is Doug Williams available?" Bizzy asked, looking around. She held her photo album close to her.

"Think so, but let me check." She picked up the phone. "Woman here to see you, Doug."

"Tell him it's Bizzy Devlin. He knows me."

The young policewoman winked. Bizzy shook her head and rolled her eyes.

Loud footsteps echoed down the hall, and Doug, dressed in a navy suit, waltzed into the waiting area. She smiled when she saw him, and he smiled back. *Strange, he doesn't usually smile.*

"Come this way, Bizzy." He opened a little gate that had been installed since the last time she had been there.

She looked down at the gate. "New?"

All the uniforms standing behind him laughed. "Yeah," said Doug. "We asked for a barrier after an incident where someone drunk came in and rushed one of our guys. This is what we got."

It made a loud squeaking noise after it closed. "Very smooth and quiet." Bizzy grinned. "I can see the town took your request very seriously."

Doug just shook his head and motioned for her to go down the hall to a small office.

"Nice," Bizzy said. "Feels very 1950 Janitor."

"How'd you know?" He walked around a desk. "Have a seat." He motioned for her to sit. She did.

"I brought you the photos of the crime scene that I shot the other day." She slid Doug a USB thumb drive.

"Thanks, Bizzy. The new guy is still in training. I'm sure your photos are more complete."

"Happy to help out." She paused and looked at him. "Doug, is Edy a person of interest?"

"Everyone is of interest until we know they had nothing

to do with it. You, of all people, know that."

"Well, I know Edy could never do anything like that."

"I didn't say she had. Did she say something to you?"

"I didn't even know Tony existed until Luigi dug up the body."

"She never told you about him?" Doug reached for his notepad.

"Never." *Crap, I shouldn't have said that.*

He opened the notepad. "How long have you two been friends?"

She went to open her mouth. Then she stopped and licked her lips. "I think this was a very painful incident. She lost Tony and..."

"Maybe she was fed up with him. Wanted him out."

"That's not what happened."

"Bizzy, what you have is what she said. And you have to admit, as her friend, you can't exactly be objective."

"As her friend, I know she's not the kind of person who could have done it."

"We have to consider every possibility, Bizzy. You worked for us long enough. You know how this works. People are full of surprises."

"Yes, I was your crime scene photographer."

"And you were good."

She stared at him. His blond hair had a few grey highlights around the edges. And even though his manner was no-nonsense, even brusque at times, what she remembered about his deep blue eyes was that there was compassion in them.

"I was okay. You know..." She didn't finish. Bizzy was a good forensic photographer, and Doug knew it. She was grateful Doug didn't bring up the big case she "blew".

The lull in the conversation led to a bit of awkwardness.

Bizzy fidgeted. She finally got up and walked to the door. "I don't believe Edy could do anything like this. Not hit someone on the head. And certainly not kill anyone."

"I hope you're right."

She walked out and then came back. "Did you talk to the warden?"

"Mr. Tuttle was the jail administrator, and we tried. He died four years ago. We did track down a prisoner in the jail reports. He was in jail awaiting his hearing at the time Tony was killed."

"Who's that?"

Doug put on his cheaters, his reading glasses. "A guy by the name of Donny Smith. Apparently, he's alive and well in Quincy."

"You will check him out, right?" Bizzy urged.

"We will follow every lead, Bizzy. But remember, Edy herself said she and Tony had an intimate relationship, and sometimes in the heat of passion, things get out of control."

Bizzy stood there for a moment. Doug looked up from the papers on his desk and looked straight at her. "Bizzy, just let us do our work and stay out of this. If the killer is still out there, he or she won't take kindly to you digging into it. You could get hurt."

"I appreciate your concern, Doug."

"But..."

Bizzy smiled. *But if my friend is your main suspect, there is no way I am going to leave this alone.*

She left. Her rubber soles made a squeaking sound as she walked down the hall. The young blonde policewoman watched her leave, and waved.

Bizzy waved back. Once she got outside, she took a couple of very deep breaths. *Damn. They* do *think it was Edy. I'm going to have to find out who did it.*

CHAPTER TEN

Bizzy walked Luigi when she came back from the police station. They had played for a while on the beach, but she was distracted. At one point, Luigi just picked up his ball, walked up the ramp, and went back to the house, leaving Bizzy on her own. Almost as if to say, "Mom, if you're not going to put your all into fetch, I don't want to play." Bizzy ran back up to the house and let him in.

"Sorry, little guy." He went in and lapped up a significant amount of water as she put the kettle on for tea. "I'll make it up to you."

A million ideas rattled in her head. She searched for paper in one of the drawers. Nothing. *I have to sketch this out. I have to put it on paper.*

Opening the fridge, she searched for something to nosh on. She picked up a bottle of ketchup. She wished she could make chocolate materialize and made a mental note to put that on the shopping list. She went to the side of the fridge to add it to the magnetic white board that she used for shopping and other to-do notes. She and Dan had used it for communication. "At a job" she had written in black scrawl, and he'd write underneath, "Where?" She answered beneath, "Shooting Gloria Mendez and her family at the park."

"You know Biz, people might not understand that note," Dan said one time as he erased a "shooting" message. "They might not know that 'shooting' means 'photographing.'"

Bizzy thought about it for a second and nearly choked on her laughter. "But *you* know."

Right now the white board was clean. No notes. She stared at Luigi. "Did you clean this off?"

Jacko had lived there just a couple of days, and she already realized he was organized and neat. And he cooked. *And he said he'd do the shopping. Bonus.*

The blank board stared back at her. She found herself writing the word "SUSPECTS" at the top. Then she wrote "Angela" on the far left. She wrote "Edy" on the right. As soon as she wrote it, she erased it.

Edy didn't do it. I won't put her on. But they were romantically involved. What is it that Doug said, and she knew it to be true? It's usually the spouse or the lover who did it. She wrote Edy's name back up on the board over on the right in very small letters. Donny Smith? She wrote his name up on the board, next to Angela.

Who else? Did Angela have a jealous hubby? Did he think Angela was cheating on him?

Someone at the jail? *Yeah, it wasn't the big house, but it still had few bad people.* She wrote jail, then a question mark. Prisoner? Guard?

"This is police business" she heard Doug say over and over in her mind as she stared at the board. His voice now looped in with every name she wrote.

Doug's tone of voice had scared her. She also knew that

he only had eyes on Edy for a suspect. *Yes, she was the easy suspect.*

Her heart ached for her friend. At first she had been upset, and even a little angry, when she found out about this big part of Edy's life she knew nothing about. Does that make her a suspect? Bizzy told her nearly everything about Dan, but there were things she kept hidden, too. Mistakes, things she may not have been proud about. The real reason she left forensic photography. Only Dan and Doug really knew about that.

Luigi lay at the door resting, but he had one eye open. *Hah, little guy, you're keeping one eye on me.* She laughed a little. Back to the suspect board, and now she wrote "MOTIVE". *Okay, why do you murder a county jail guard?*

She recounted what Edy had said before he went missing. Odd shifts. Working the third shift when he didn't normally do that. Why?

The administrator or warden had died years ago. Who else would know?

Oh, crap. No, I can't ask him. Get it out of your head, Bizzy. Not him.

Luigi's head went to attention, and then he jumped up. He started to bark and whine.

"What's up, Luigi?"

The door opened, and Jacko walked in laden with grocery bags.

"It's me, Luigi. Uncle Jacko."

Luigi ran around jumping and barking, then jumped some more. He ran over to get a ball. He found one and ran back to Jacko. *Poor guy is desperate for a game of fetch.*

Bizzy reached for a couple of the bags. "By any chance did you buy chocolate?"

"Yes. You had it on the board three times."

"Oh, thank God!"

Jacko glanced over to the white board. "I cleaned that-"

"You did. I was writing a suspect/motive board."

"A what?"

"I should probably put 'means,' too." She went to the board and wrote "MEANS," but the dry erase pen squeaked a little as she wrote it, and Luigi barked.

Jacko read the names, then turned to Bizzy. "Angela, I know. Who is Donny?"

"Donny Smith was a prisoner in the jail at the same time Tony was there."

"You think he's a suspect?"

"I'm not sure. Doug Williams mentioned him in passing."

"When?"

"Earlier today when I went to see him."

"You went to see Dougie?"

"Right."

"Why did you go to see him?"

"I took him my photos of the crime scene. But mostly I wanted to know why he was so convinced that Edy is the *only* suspect. Jacko, he's not even *looking* at other people. Not really."

"They've just started the investigation."

They both unpacked the bags full of groceries and started putting things away. Bizzy found three large chocolate bars, put them up to her nose, and inhaled. "Hello, my little friends."

"What do you think of spaghetti carbonara tonight?"

"Seriously?"

"You don't like it?"

"I *love* it." Bizzy had to stop herself from jumping up and down with glee.

"Good, because I got all *gli ingredienti*." His Italian slipped out with the last words.

She stared at Jacko for a moment. The idea popped back into her brain. *Oh no, Bizzy, get it out of your head.*

"Uh oh, what? What's that face for?" Jacko asked.

"Oh man." She picked up the loaf of crusty bread, squeezing it a little.

"Don't squeeze the *pane.*"

"What would you think if I offered Schaeffer a free photo session with Wolf?"

He just looked at her, went to one of the cabinets, and put some cans of tomatoes away. "You don't like him very much."

"He's my neighbor."

"Yeah, but—"

"I figured I would offer that, and maybe ask him a few questions about Tony and the jail."

"Oh boy, Bizzy."

"Listen, I'm not letting my friend get arrested for murder. Just not happening. The police are fixated on her. Just *her.*"

"So you go over and ask Schaeffer questions, and he gets mad."

"Maybe he'll get mad. It's just an excuse so I can ask questions."

"That you shouldn't be asking."

Bizzy had already picked up the leash and walked in Luigi's direction.

"Why are you taking him with you?"

"Moral support."

"You want me to go?" Jacko asked.

"No." Bizzy twisted Luigi's collar to attach the leash. "I

think if we both went, Schaeffer might be suspicious. Plus," she opened the door, "I'm starving."

BIZZY STARED down the trail of obstacles that Schaeffer had strewn along the path to his front door over the years. Luigi pulled her along, sniffing everything and occasionally lifting his leg to spritz an object. "Wolf is not going to be your friend if you keep marking his property, and Schaeffer will *definitely* not like you."

Still Luigi went to the next pile of junk and raised his leg.

"Remember," she whispered to the dog, "you're here for moral support. And be excited when I ask Wolf to be a model."

Luigi gave her a sideways glance but trotted right beside her.

They passed Schaeffer's unfinished projects, junk rescued from the beach, and a fair number of old lobster traps - the ones with wood and wire and those that would be sure to hurt someone walking up this path. *Probably what he wants.* Compared to the newer kind, with plastic covering over the metal mesh, these looked like death traps for both the lobster and anyone who accidentally brushed up against one. She'd never actually walked through this path to Schaeffer's house, mainly because she was a little afraid of him. *Everybody* was a little afraid of Schaeffer. Edy said he had been nice once upon a time. Bizzy remembered his property being cute, the junk arranged in a cute beachy way. Then he stopped taking care of it.

She walked about a quarter of the way through the succession of junk, when her gray sweatpants caught on a jagged piece of a lobster trap. It tore a little hole in her sweatpants, but Bizzy kept going. *I'm glad these are old. I was going to throw them out, anyway.* She had worn her oldest, most worn pair of sweat pants in case this happened. She wore them around the house all the time and knew they would wear out soon.

Stacked at one point along the path were a bunch of small dinghies, all nearly fallen apart. She imagined someone taking one out on the ocean and shuddered.

The cottage itself looked as if it should be condemned. Shingles from both the side and the roof were missing. In some places, the shingles were replaced by pieces of old black tar paper, generally used as an extra layer of protection beneath shingles. The old shingles must have been blue at one point, but now they were well faded. She stood outside the worn, chipping door, afraid to knock. A big sign in red ink said: "No soliciting, No Jehovah's Witnesses." In fact, it actually said, "Don't knock."

Luigi sniffed everything around the door, his little heart-shaped nose working overtime. Bizzy noticed a strange smell, but when she looked around, she saw in the corner of the yard a small garden full of wildflowers still blooming in late summer, almost fall. Some fresh mulch had been placed around the garden. *That's it. The mulch. It just smells so bad.* Luigi picked that moment to lift his leg and squirt on a broken gnome by the door.

At first she heard the sound but couldn't place it. A growl? Schaeffer or Wolf?

She could hear it better now. A low, menacing growl on the other side of the door getting louder and louder. Schaeffer's dog, Wolf, did not play with other dogs, and Schaeffer didn't walk him around the neighborhood like all the other dog owners. Wolf had a reputation, and Schaeffer had numerous animal control citations for the times Wolf had accidentally gotten out and scared the neighbors. His main crime, though, was that Wolf loved to tear apart trash cans. Schaeffer would take him for nighttime strolls on the beach. Sometimes, on a full moon, he and Schaeffer looked like man and bear walking along the water's edge.

The growling got louder. Bizzy glanced down at Luigi, who now hid behind her, his little sweet face popping out between her knees.

Bizzy looked down at her canine companion. "I'm scared, too, buddy."

Taking a deep breath, she raised her hand and knocked. Wolf started barking now. Mean barking. I'm-going-to-attack-you barking. Bizzy regretted bringing Luigi. He cowered beside her, whimpering.

From inside she could hear Schaeffer yelling at the dog. "Shut up, Wolf. Quiet!" Wolf just barked louder. Now she felt her puppy shaking behind her. She heard footsteps along with the barking, but she wasn't sure. She knocked again.

"Who's there?" Schaeffer growled over the dog's whining.

Now Wolf's barking took on a new, more furious tone, mirroring his master's demeanor. She heard stomping coming her way.

"Who's there?" he shouted.

"Bizzy. Bizzy Devlin, Mr. Schaeffer." She tried to sound confident and polite. The polite part was the hard part.

"Who?" He had to yell just to be heard over his dog's barking.

"Your neighbor, Bizzy Devlin," she called out. *He knows who I am.*

It took Schaeffer great effort to open the heavily warped

door. It creaked loudly. More than a few paint chips fell from the door to the ground.

Schaeffer stood around 5'10," burley, with his signature Hawaiian shirt on, open down the front, and a stained white t-shirt hugging his prominent belly. He put his hand up on the doorway, but didn't open the ripped screen door.

"What'd you want?"

"I wanted to ask you something."

He glared at her through the broken screen door. She noticed a big gash at the bottom, where Bizzy speculated that Wolf might have tried to escape. And, by the looks of it, may have been successful.

She looked down at her petrified puppy. *If we have to make a run for it, I'll pick you up.*

"I have a small proposal for you." She took a big deep breath. "I am starting a new portraiture line for my business, and Wolf would make great model for me. I would give you photos for free. I would shoot him here or in the studio, and I would give you a free print." The last sentence came out rapid fire and nervous. She wondered how many times she had said *free*.

Wolf stuck his head out the hole in the screen door, his mouth in a snarl.

Bizzy stepped back, almost stepping on Luigi. "I really would like to have a whole assortment of different breeds. And I would like Wolf -"

Schaeffer snorted. "Ya think this guy would sit for a portrait?" Then he started to laugh his gravelly laugh and patted Wolf on the head. "This guy would eat your camera." Wolf sat down at the door proudly when his owner said that.

"I think Wolf is a regal dog, and I love his coloring, and I think he'd make a beautiful portrait subject." Still nervous.

Still rapid fire, but she meant it. She had a special place in her heart for Rotties. Her best friend growing up had one named Hera, and she remembered Hera snuggled up to her on every sleepover. Hera had simply been one of the sweetest dogs she had ever met.

Schaeffer's deep brown eyes fixated on her, softening a little.

"I'll think on it."

"It's for free," she quickly added again. Bizzy wasn't sure that mattered to a man like Bertie Schaeffer, but it was worth a try. "And-"

"I said I'd think on it." Back to his cranky self.

They continued to stare at each other. *Ask. Ask the questions.*

"You know about the skeleton they found between me and Edy's house, right?" He knew about the finding of the bones. He had been there, asking questions, prying.

"Yup."

"Did you know that it was Tony Giancarlo?"

He raised his eyebrows.

He didn't know. "Did you know?" she asked again.

"*Now* I know. Hadn't heard before this." His voice changed a little. He looked down at Wolf.

"You knew him, right?"

"Yup."

The dog had a low growl, and Schaeffer was barely holding him back. "Nice Wolf," Bizzy said in a soft voice, staring down the menacing canine. "You are a beautiful dog, Wolfie."

"Stop growling." He patted him on the head and held his collar.

"Maybe he and Luigi could play sometime."

"My dog doesn't like other dogs. *I* don't like other dogs." He glared at Luigi, now completely cowering behind her.

She nodded. "Do you happen to remember when we replaced the deck? Dan and Edy's son, Jay did it."

"Did it without a permit. I remember."

"Actually we did it *with* a permit, because you made sure to call the building inspector, and he approved it."

He snorted at this. "You better have a permit for *that*." He pointed over toward Bizzy's house.

"Yes, we do," she said. "From Conservation, too. And you know that." All this politeness towards Schaeffer now gave her a headache.

"Too much building."

"If I don't fix the house, it will fall down." She said the last part very softly. "Dan would hate that."

Schaeffer shrugged.

"Remember when we built the deck and you came over, after we had the permit, and you gave Dan lots of advice?" Schaeffer had given them *lots* and lots of advice. On one particular occasion, Dan said that Schaeffer's "advice" might have saved them some time and money, but otherwise Dan mostly had a headache from Schaeffer's meddling.

"Yeah, Dan didn't really know what he was doing."

Bizzy felt a mixture of anger and hurt. *Not the time to lash out.* "Right, and you helped quite a lot. Dan said you saved him some time and money." *Patience. Patience.*

"Dan was an okay guy."

"You remember the project at all? Do you remember when we picked up all the old wood-"

"Some of it was still good. But you didn't use it. Should have given it to me."

Bizzy knew most of it had been rotten and unusable.

"Right. I think they used some," she lied. They had paid a pretty penny to have it all carted away.

"Right." He was back to monosyllabic answers.

"You remember anything odd about the sand? You took some photos of us. Remember?"

"Nothing."

Two syllables.

"Why?" Schaeffer asked. He was still holding on to the dog, and even through the screen, Bizzy could see Wolfie frothing at the mouth. Luigi still cowered behind her.

"Nothing." A thought came to her. "How long did you work at the old Pullen Pointe Jail? You worked with Tony, right?"

"Yup."

"How long?"

"Almost 40 years. Not all that time with Tony. I was older than he was."

"What was the jail like?"

"It was a jail. Cold and nasty. The way it should be. Now they're like hotels. They coddle the prisoners."

"Did you go to the new place when they moved?"

"Thought about it. Had to travel too far. Didn't like leaving Jeannie-" He stopped.

"Were you and Tony friends?" Bizzy finally got to the question she had wanted to ask all along.

"Not really."

"But you worked together. And were neighbors."

"Yeah, I worked with a lot of people I wasn't friends with. Why you want to know?" Wolf laid down in front of the door. She guessed standing guard had tired him out. Luigi also had laid down behind her, but with his head now resting right behind her ankles.

"Just trying to find out what was going on with the guy who was buried on my property."

"It's *Edith's* property. Not yours."

"Well, it was between our houses."

"It's Edith's property."

Bizzy knew he was right.

"Was Tony nice? Did you like him?"

He glared at her. "He was okay. I wouldn't date him." He laughed, snorted at his own joke. "He wasn't good at his job. Kinda a bad guard."

"He was?"

"Yeah, too soft. Too chummy with some of the prisoners. I told the police. Not a good guard."

"That's not what I heard. Did Edy know?"

"He probably had her fooled. Maybe not, though. I heard he was a ladies' man."

"He was?"

"Sure. Heard them fighting about it. All the windows open, and she's screaming about some woman."

"I find that hard-"

"Believe it. Tony was *not* a good guy. Why you asking?"

"I'm still a little bit in shock about the remains being found so close to my house."

"Who knows? Maybe one of the jail prisoners killed him."

"How would you know that?"

"Just speculating. Fred Long might know more than me. They talked more. Old Fred knew more than I did about the ins and outs of the jail. Friends with everyone. We called him the mayor." He laughed a little at that.

Yeah, Fred Long is a lot nicer than you.

She nudged Luigi a little, who hadn't moved in the entire time she had been talking to Schaeffer. He opened his eyes, but still his body remained frozen. *He's playing dead.*

"Also, Edy had a serious temper. I remember her yelling at that kid, too. Hey, I like Edy. She's a good woman. Always nice to me. And Jeannie. The kid was a real rebel. That kid needed some yelling at."

"You think she could kill Tony?" They played their staring game again.

"If I were a betting man, I'd say no. I think she loved him. She's the type of woman who loves a guy no matter what." Bizzy wondered if maybe he was talking about Jeannie, his deceased wife, and less about Edy. "I think he was up to something in that jail. Probably no good."

"But you're not sure?" Bizzy asked.

He shook his head. "That's just something I heard when he went missing." He pulled back Wolf. "Also, Angela, was one of the girls who worked at the prison."

"What?"

"Worked for the Warden, if I remember right. Not sure I remember right anymore, though." With that he shut the door. More paint chips fluttered to the ground.

CHAPTER ELEVEN

"So what do you think, Jacko?" Bizzy asked as she watched him finish making dinner.

The place smelled of bacon. *This is what heaven smells like.* Jacko jumped from stove to sink and back again to the stove. It looked like dancing, except his dance partner was a colander of hot spaghetti. He dumped the spaghetti in with the fried bacon and covered it with the bacon drippings and chips of bacon remaining in the pan. In another dish all the bacon lay crisp and waiting.

She told him what Schaeffer said about Tony being a bad guard.

"There is stuff that goes on in jails that I never want to know about." He whisked some egg yolks.

Luigi retrieved a ball from his overflowing toy box and nudged Jacko with it. They had developed an indoor fetch game in the short time since Jacko had moved in. Luigi would fetch the ball and stick it into the back of Jacko's knees. Then Jacko placed whatever cooking utensil he held on the counter, tug the ball from Luigi's mouth, and gently throw the ball somewhere in the small living room. After a quick rinse of his hands, Jacko went back to cooking as Luigi ran to retrieve the ball. And then the whole thing began again.

"I don't know who enjoys the playing more - you or Luigi," Bizzy said.

"I always wanted a dog. I almost," he put his thumb and index finger an inch apart, "*almost* got one from my parents. But my dad said no. Too much work. He said I wasn't responsible enough."

"How old were you?" asked Bizzy, walking into the living room.

"Ten."

"Yeah, your mom would have had to do all the work," Bizzy said. She saw a look of hurt come across Jacko's face. "But a boy *does* need a dog. And now you have one!"

"Started putting out feelers for the pet photography." On cue, Luigi nudged him with the orange ball.

"I guess we do it the way we do for people portraits."

"We should run a voucher program or something." Jacko threw cheese and other stuff in with the eggs. "Actually I was talking to a guy today. He said he wanted a portrait of his dog on the beach."

"That's great. We'll get some owners to pose with their pets. It could be fun. Hey, maybe we should have costumes for the pets and owners!" Bizzy laughed.

Jacko let go of the ball. "That's enough, Luigi." The dog, of course, didn't know what that meant.

"About to 'squirrel' on you," Bizzy said, going back into the kitchen. "Schaeffer seemed pretty convinced that Tony had something going on at the jail."

"But he didn't know what?" Jacko asked.

"Right." Bizzy watched Jacko stir in the egg and cheese

until it became creamy, and he helped it along with a little pasta water.

"Just from what I've seen on TV and films, jail is not a great place to be." Jacko opened a cabinet. "Where are your pasta bowls?"

"You mean just bowls, right? I'll set up the TV tables for dinner." She turned around in the cramped kitchen. "Soon the kitchen will be bigger, and there will be a place to eat in here. And I will love it even more than I do now." She shut her eyes.

"Hey, you okay?" Jacko asked.

"I'm visualizing. Seeing the open concept with all the cabinets I need. And everything is white."

"I'd open my eyes if I were you, because dinner is ready." Jacko chuckled.

Bizzy inhaled deeply. "So what do you think?"

"About the food, visualization, open concepts-"

"What Schaeffer said." Bizzy opened her eyes.

"I think it's been a long time. How old is he?"

"Not sure."

"Well it's been 25 years since Tony went missing." Jacko opened one cabinet, then another. "So where are your bowls?"

She pointed. "The bowls are in the cabinet just to the left of the one above the sink." Jacko went over and got them.

"Glasses, silverware?"

Bizzy pointed to another cabinet.

"I don't have any wine or anything. I don't really drink it anymore," she said.

"Water is fine. You have that, right?" He smiled.

"Yes, I do. The finest Pullen Pointe has to offer."

"Did you live here when the jail was here?" Jacko returned to the subject Bizzy was most eager to discuss.

"It was closed and torn down long before I came on the scene. But people still talked about it."

"Did Schaeffer always live here?"

"Yeah. Fred Long, too. The way Dan told it, at one time this whole neighborhood was home to mostly jail and airline personnel."

"Must have been a hopping place to be." He smiled and filled up two glasses with water, placing them on the TV tables in the adjacent living room.

Bizzy stood over the stove and took in a long whiff of the pasta carbonara. "Smells fantastic."

Jacko nodded. "Haven't had that many complaints. Do you mind my cooking sometimes?" he asked as he put the bowls on the tables. He then went back to get the bread.

She turned, pulling out a bread knife and pointing at him. "You can cook for me for the rest of your life."

He smiled. "Glad to hear it. I really like to cook."

"I might talk to Fred. Schaeffer called him 'the mayor,'" she said, sitting down in front of her dinner. "He's a nice guy."

"Meanwhile, I hope the guy I talked to today calls. His name is Tom. I told him I lived down here at the Pointe, and he said he knew of you."

Bizzy watched as Jacko put his pasta creation into bowls. "How'd he know of me?"

"Don't know." He picked up his fork and spoon and began to twirl the pasta on the spoon. "Anyway, I'll put out a voucher advertisement for Thursday. Our big experiment — I hope it works."

"I hope people show up." Bizzy twirled her pasta on the

big spoon just like Jacko did. "Jacko, if I try to eat pasta like this, I'm gonna starve. This is like chopsticks."

◦∼◦

BIZZY HEARD a faint knock on the door, and when she pulled her watch to her face and pried open her eyes, she saw that the time was barely 5:45 a.m. Luigi, who had stayed on the floor in his own bed, looked at her, his eyes barely open. The faint knock rapped again. He barked a little, coupled by a little growl.

The knock was louder now. *Or am I'm just more awake?* Bizzy wondered drowsily. She lifted the window shade up but couldn't see anything at the door. Next, she put a sweatshirt on over her PJs and left her room. She saw Jacko's door was closed.

"Jacko," she whispered.

She put her ear against his door but only heard a low snoring.

This time the knock was forceful. She opened Jacko's door and peeked in. He was sprawled out on the bed. Luigi jumped up on the bed and began to lick his face.

"What?" Jacko realized it was the dog giving him a thorough face cleaning.

"Luigi, what are -"

"Jacko," she said as she stood at the foot of the bed, "someone is at the door."

He jumped up and grabbed his jeans off the back of the chair.

"Who is it? Is something wrong?" he asked half asleep.

"I don't know. But it's 5:45 a.m."

"Who would come to the house at this hour?"

She nodded. "Right. Who?"

They stood there looking at each other.

"I guess we have to answer the door."

They both heard the noise, and Luigi ran down the stairs barking with a little growl.

"Luigi, is that you?"

The sound came again and sounded like a bark. But it was low and faint, so they couldn't make out the noise for sure. Luigi, now at the door, barked furiously at whatever was outside.

Jacko and Bizzy walked toward the door, and Jacko went first to open it.

A tall, very lanky man stood there. His face had a gaunt, grayish look, and he wore a tweed Irish cap over his eyes. His jeans had a dirty, crumpled look, and what looked like a 1980s windbreaker. He smiled when Jacko opened the door. When the man saw Bizzy, he removed his cap.

"We're here," he said in a very low voice, almost a whisper.

Did I forget something? Did Howie have something scheduled for the renovations?

Bizzy caught sight of an enormous creature next to the man with the cap. It was a massive fawn-colored dog.

"Tom?" Jacko barely got the name out.

"You said that the best time in the morning for a picture was dawn."

Bizzy looked at the dog. Luigi looked like a Chihuahua in comparison to this enormous dog.

"Good morning, ma'am. You must be Bizzy."

"Yes."

"Tom." Jacko looked over to Bizzy and then back at Tom. "Did we make an appointment for now?"

"No, but I checked the weather. And today is the best

day out of the next couple. Figured we'd get it done today and not have to worry about it."

"Right," Jacko said.

All three of them stood there.

"You know," Tom said glancing around the yard, "you could put a nice deck here." He pointed to the sand still littered with a few yellow bits of tape. "Be so much easier to walk out here."

Bizzy nodded, "You're right. Would you like to come in?"

He patted his dog. "Might be best if we remained outside. Tom, Jr. and I don't mind waiting."

"Okay, we're going to close the door so Luigi doesn't get out or bark."

"No problem," he said. He spotted one of the plastic chairs and sat in it. Tom, Jr. followed him and lay at his feet.

Bizzy ran over to the coffee machine, took the pot and filled it with water, and poured the water in the machine.

"Do we have time for coffee?" Jacko asked.

She stopped, coffee filter and a bag of coffee in hand. "We *make* time for coffee." Bizzy made sure everything was ready and pressed the *on* switch.

"I'm going to put clothes on." She dashed to the stairs, but stopped to watch the dog out the window.

"Bizzy, I swear, I didn't tell him to come at this time."

She watched as the dog licked its big paw. "That's a Newfoundland, isn't it?"

"It seems like a nice dog. A gentle giant," Jacko said.

"It's a bear. And he named the dog after himself," Bizzy whispered as the coffee maker went into full brewing, gurgling, and hissing sounds.

"I know."

"I'll be right back." She dashed up the stairs and in five

minutes came back down in jeans, a long sleeve t-shirt, and her hair in a ponytail.

Jacko poured two cups of coffee in plastic to-go cups. "I asked him if he wanted coffee, but he said no."

Two cameras were on the counter. "They're ready?" she asked.

"Clean cards, date/name format, and fully charged batteries."

She went over to the to-go cup of coffee. "You ready?"

"Two seconds."

He ran upstairs, and she could hear him stomping around before he came back down.

She put her cream and sugar in, blew on it, then took a small sip.

"Edy's up," he said as he put one of the cameras around his neck and placed a reflector under his arm.

"I'm going to ask her to mind Luigi."

Edy said yes, but her eyes were swollen from lack of sleep. Bizzy told her there was a fresh pot of coffee over at her house, but Edy declined.

"Just give me the puppy," she said. "I need something furry and warm to cuddle with."

The sun was due to come up about 6:30 a.m., and it was now close to 6:10.

She had a camera around her neck and a flash in her jacket pocket.

Tom and Tom, Jr. walked behind them. The dog lumbered. *In fact, "lumbered" might be too fast a description of his gait.*

"I had this idea," human Tom said, "that maybe Tom, Jr. could run in the waves."

Bizzy saw the animal beside his owner. *This dog is not a*

runner. Luigi ran and bounded like a gazelle. He skimmed the waves. *Tom, Jr., not a gazelle.*

"Let's get to the water's edge." Bizzy moved quickly to the water, which unluckily for her was at low tide. She calculated it would take an additional five minutes for the slow-moving Tom, Jr., who Tom called "TJ", to reach the water's edge.

They finally made it, and Jacko ran along the water's edges to get TJ to run in the water. TJ huffed at him. Didn't even bark.

"I think you're making TJ laugh with your weird running," Bizzy laughed.

"Now, boy," Tom encouraged TJ, "why don't you go get in the water?" Tom walked to the edge, and his dog followed. "Don't you want to swim in the ocean?"

"Does he swim?"

"Not really. Thought he might for this picture."

"Do you have any treats, Tom?"

He pulled a small plastic tub out of his pocket. "It's his food, but it's also his treats."

"Okay, let's see what we can do with these." Jacko took the treats and went to the water's edge. TJ bounded behind him, reaching for the treats, though Jacko didn't notice the dog behind him.

"Jacko watch-" just as she said it TJ tackled Jacko, and the two of them tumbled into the water.

Bizzy took as many photos as she could. She turned the camera and put on it continuous focus, a setting she used for sports shots. Jacko got up and ran down the beach with TJ chasing him, albeit slowly.

At one point TJ turned to Bizzy because of the clicking sound, but the lure of the treats in Jacko's hands refocused him. The sun broke on the horizon, and TJ landed square in the lone beam of sunlight stretching over the water to the edge of the beach. He looked like a bear running, but human Tom giggled and cheered him on.

"That's my boy!"

Jacko, dripping, came back when the treats were all eaten. "The water is freezing. I'm freezing."

"Are you okay?" Bizzy asked.

Jacko nodded. They both turned to see Tom and TJ sitting on the beach. Tom stroked the side of TJ's body, and the dog nuzzled up to his human's face. Both gazed at each other with pure love. Bizzy pushed the shutter once more.

That's the photo. Father and son.

CHAPTER TWELVE

"Apparently, we have a voucher client for our pet photography," Jacko said as he sniffed the pot of food Bizzy was preparing on the stove later that day. "Hmmmm... Clearly you are a lover of garlic. A girl after my own Italian heart."

Bizzy added more salt and a little oregano, then stirred. "We haven't even done any advertising." She scooped up some of the dinner concoction from the steaming pot and served them both, setting the bowls on the TV dinner tables. They were both hungry and dug in.

"Yum. This is good! What's it called?"

"Musgo stew," Bizzy replied. "And look," she said pointing to the green noodles, "I made zoodles. Healthy alternative to pasta."

Jacko looked at her with a puzzled look. "What is musgo stew, and what is a zoodle?"

"Whatever is still in the fridge by Thursday must go. And a zoodle is just a zucchini noodle," Bizzy said. "You might want to top it off with some Parmesan cheese."

Jacko shook some cheese onto the stew and sniffed. "My

compliments to the chef. Smells delicious. Hey, did the carbonara go in here?"

Bizzy smiled and sucked in a zoodle. "I ate that for breakfast." Between mouthfuls, Bizzy asked, "I think we've done a great job with the animals we've photographed so far, but is there anything different about pet photography?"

"Well, I'm betting it's a lot like people. Except instead of cheese and crackers for snacks, we use pet treats." Bizzy always liked to have snacks available for her clients. Fruit, nuts, coffee, sparkling water, and, for the special client, maybe a little bubbly.

Bizzy smiled. "Well that sounds simple enough. Who is the dog?"

"Apollo, the Bullmastiff."

"And who is the human component?"

"Not sure who the human is. He said he received a voucher and was coming and Apollo was the dog's name."

Bizzy nearly choked on a mouthful of the stew as she laughed. "He said he was making an appointment for Apollo?"

"I'm going to have to get used to this pet stuff. I think he did leave a last name."

The two of them laughed.

"When's the shoot?" asked Bizzy.

"Tomorrow at 10:30. Apparently Apollo's best times are between 10 to 12. The human has another appointment somewhere at 9:30, but he said he would come right over after that."

"All this info and he never left his name." Jacko shrugged. "I'll have to ask Edy if she'll let Luigi out."

"Sounds good." Jacko smiled. "I wonder if it's like Tom and TJ. Maybe the owner named the dog after him. I mean, is this a trend? Owners naming dogs after themselves?"

"Remind me again who I named Luigi after?"

"My grandfather. And you said you liked the name."

Bizzy smiled. "Going over to Edy's real quick."

"It's never quick when you go over there. But she can probably use a friendly shoulder right now. I'll clean up around here." He peered at all the dishes and pots and pans. "And this was a *leftover* meal?"

Bizzy flew out the door without looking back. She called in through Edy's screen door. "Knock, knock!"

She could see the brief outline of Edy frozen like a statue on her chair. "Hey Edy, can I come in?"

Edy turned to her and dabbed a tissue to her eye.

"Ok, Edy, I'm coming in. Something's wrong."

Her friend sat in an old fluffy wicker chair. Edy had bought it at a flea market, fixed it up, and made new cushion covers for it. Right now the cushions had bright red lobsters on them. But Bizzy knew that would change as soon as the mood came across Edy. Last time it was whales.

"What's going on?" Bizzy plopped down across from her friend on the matching ottoman.

Edy's breathed unevenly, not quite crying. "Just remembering."

"About Tony?"

Edy nodded. "Just trying to remember everything, how it went down. I'm searching right now for a diary I kept around that time. I know I wrote down my thoughts, feelings. What he said to me. I'm going to be arrested for his murder. Doug as much as said so."

Bizzy had to catch her breath. "What do you remember right now about that time? About Tony?"

"Something was going on at the jail," Edy said.

"What?" Bizzy asked.

Edy pulled the last tissue out of the box. And Bizzy looked around to see if she could find another.

She could see a box in the small bathroom off the hall, and she stood up to get it.

"We were in love," she said, "but I was scared."

"Why?"

"Bizzy, if you haven't noticed, I'm black."

"Wasn't that the eighties, nineties?"

Edy looked at her. "Honey, racism is still going on today, and at the time it wasn't that far removed from the civil rights sixties, and the school desegregation seventies here in Boston."

Bizzy hung her head. "Yeah, you're right, I don't remember that much from back then."

"Of course not. You were still a baby."

"Not a *baby*. A kid, almost a teen."

"He felt his family wouldn't accept me. Us."

They sat there. Edy stared at the gas fireplace. "I wish it were a little colder, so I could turn that thing on."

Bizzy chuckled. "We can still turn it on if you want. Nothing says it has to be cold out."

Edy turned to Bizzy and said, "All these years I thought he left me because his family wouldn't accept me."

"But he didn't." Bizzy reached out and grabbed her hand.

"I said 'never again'. For *any* man. No matter what the color. 'No more,' I said."

"Oh, Edy!" Bizzy started to tear up as well and grabbed a tissue.

"The police come by again today, and they asked me if I knew about a woman named Angela. That's when I knew."

"Did you?"

"At first I didn't remember. But then it kind of came back to me."

"Who was she? Schaeffer mentioned her, too."

"She worked at the jail. And she called Tony here." Edy raised her eyebrows. "I used to have a landline and an answering machine, and she left a couple of messages."

"What did they say?"

She groaned. "I was really jealous of her for some reason."

"What did she say on these messages?"

"Just for him to call her back, mostly." She sniffled again. For Bizzy, it was like seeing Wonder Woman in tears. Edy had always been a rock, a beacon of hope for her in her times of need.

"And..."

"And what?"

Bizzy looked at her friend and grabbed her hand. "Something has you scared, Edy."

"I thought he might be having an affair."

Bizzy looked at her. "And *was* he?"

"I don't know."

"Did you *ask* him?" Bizzy tried to quell both the fear and anger bubbling up inside her. Fear for her friend, and anger at Tony, whom she never knew, if he had been cheating on her best friend.

"I did. He said no way. He just worked with her. But he wouldn't tell me why she was calling."

"Did you really think he was having an affair with *her*?"

"I was a different person then. Less confident. More stupid."

"Well you had Jay to think about."

"And he was so young. And I was just trying to make ends meet."

Bizzy realized the sun was going down, or maybe it was that the clouds were moving in. All of a sudden, it was very dark in the room. She got up to turn some of the lights on.

"Please don't," Edy whined.

"Oh no, young lady," Bizzy said firmly, "you wouldn't let me sit in the dark when I felt that way."

Edy leaned back in her wicker chair. "Okay. Fair enough."

"So it sounds like something was going on at the jail." Bizzy didn't look at Edy. Her mind was spinning. "I talked to Schaeffer."

"Schaeffer. What a son of a – he said some stuff to the police. It wasn't true. He said we fought all the time."

"Were they friends - Tony and Schaeffer?"

Edy shook her head. "No. First of all, Schaeffer and Tony never hit it off. And Tony thought something was off with the way Schaeffer treated the prisoners at the jail."

"Like what?"

"I don't know. He wouldn't say any more about that. As a rule, Tony didn't like to bring home any troubles he had at work."

Bizzy almost told her what Schaeffer had said to her, but she stopped. *I could see Schaeffer being involved in something shady.* "Did Tony think Schaeffer was part of something?"

"Maybe. But he never said it outright in so many words."

Bizzy sat in the chair across from Edy. "Where's that diary you were talking about?"

Edy shook her head. "Don't know. Haven't found it yet. I've been tearing this place apart for it."

"Keep going. And do you have any more photos of that time? Of Tony, or *anything*? Do you remember anything about any of the guys who worked at the jail?"

Edy turned around. "You know, at one point Tony and Fred Long were really good friends. Good friends for a while. Then they weren't."

"What came between them?"

Edy turned her with her tear-streaked cheeks. "Me."

"Long had a thing for you?"

"Did all sorts of things. Very sweet stuff. He was divorced. Twice." She chuckled now. "I guess Long was sweet. Tony didn't like it. Fred helped me with gardening all the time."

"He wants to beautify everything. He's the one who gave me those hostas your puppy destroyed."

Bizzy smiled. "Strange that he was into you, and he knew Tony was...".

"Not so strange. His wife had just divorced him, and he was alone. And he liked to teach me gardening. You might not know it from his yard now, but it used to be really beautiful. It won awards. Schaeffer's was beautiful, too. They actually shipped dirt and mulch in, and shared it."

"You learned your gardening lessons very, very well."

"I like to think so."

"Do you remember Angela's last name?"

"Gotti."

"Gotti? Like the gangster?"

"It's the only reason I remember it."

"I don't think I'm going to forget it," Bizzy said.

"Did you ever hear from her after Tony left- or -" Bizzy trailed off. She didn't feel comfortable saying "Tony is dead" in front of Edy.

"I did. She called. She didn't know he..." Edy caught her breath, "...had left, I told her he hadn't come home and that I didn't know where he went."

Bizzy's brain started twirling with possibilities. "Was that the only time?"

"Why are you so curious?"

"I wanted to know about this guy." Bizzy saw Edy's scrunched-up face, and the turmoil she felt was evident. "I wanted to know, because my closest friend in the world is in pain."

Neither woman looked at each other, and the air felt heavy and awkward to Bizzy. "Will you find that diary?"

"I'll find that diary, Biz."

"Good. Good."

"Bizzy, you said you wanted to ask me something."

"Oh, yeah, um, but maybe it's not the right time."

"What?"

"It looks like we might have a pet client tomorrow."

"Great!" Edy seemed genuinely happy about the news.

"Yeah. And I was going to ask you to let Luigi out. Apollo is a Bullmastiff. My little guy might not be able to handle that kind of power."

"Send your boy to me. I'll take good care of him."

Bizzy got up and walked toward the door. "Where did she live - Angela?"

"Twenty-five years ago in East Boston. I doubt she's there now."

CHAPTER THIRTEEN

The beeping and gurgling of the electric kettle drew Jacko to the kitchen. Bizzy sat frozen in front of her computer, every so often clicking the mouse. She had come back from Edy's and almost immediately pulled out the computer. She turned the kettle on but soon forgot about it. She sat transfixed by the words on the screen and scrolled up and down.

"You *do* hear that, right? Been going off now for a long time."

She jumped up. "Oh my yes!" She ran over to the cabinet and pulled down a mug. The mug had a cute saying on it about a dog, but it had faded, so now the only words were "bark" and "dog."

"The way you go from coffee to tea amazes me," Jacko said.

"Could you please pull out the Chinese tea Edy brought from China last year?"

"You know it *does* have a name." He pulled out a bag of tea with only Chinese labeling on it. "On second thought, maybe 'the Chinese tea Edy brought back from China Last Year' is just the perfect name."

"See? 'Chinese tea Edy brought back from China Last Year,'" Bizzy chuckled at her own joke. "Would you please pull down the tea bags, too?"

He did. Since this was a loose tea, providing a steeping bag was necessary. "I don't know. I don't mind the regular tea that comes in its own bag with a little paper tag."

Says the guy who can't stand tea.

She got up and put the tea in the bag, then let it steep in the cup. "I really like it. It's fruity."

He glanced at her screen. "What are you doing?"

"Trying to find Angela Gotti," she said while pouring the water and arranging the tea bag in the cup. She pulled the cup to her face and inhaled. "The smell is so nice."

"You think you're going to find her?"

"I've found other people this way." Bizzy liked to look up clients she didn't know before a shoot to get a general sense and background about them. When she photographed crime scenes, sometimes she'd try to find out about the people involved. That drained her emotionally, though, so she stopped. Bizzy didn't hold out much hope of actually finding Angela after so many years. But a childhood friend of Bizzy's had found *her* after 20 years, and now they were friends again.

Jacko now filled a teabag with the Chinese tea and poured the boiling water in cup. "It's been a lot of years."

"Twenty-five. It's a way to find out what was *really* happening at that jail. With Tony. It might be the only way." She sniffed the tea again. It was still too piping hot to sip.

"Can Dougie find her?"

"I don't know. Probably could if he wanted to. Don't get me wrong, he's a good cop, but he thinks he has his killer."

Jacko groaned. "He didn't tell you where she is."

"I didn't ask, Doug, because I didn't want to hear one more time how it's none of my business, and this is a police matter."

"It *isn't* your business."

Bizzy glared at him. "Yes, it is. It's Edy."

He went over and pulled his own cup off the shelf, then put it under the espresso machine. It was a small cup. And as soon it was filled, he drank it like a shot. Then he made a cup of tea.

Nothing to say to that, huh? Bizzy knew something was on his mind. "So you're having both at the same time?"

He shrugged. He carried the mug of tea into the living room.

"I'm trying to find her." She kept tapping keys, then she'd scroll, and finally she'd just sigh. "It keeps coming back to East Boston." She took a sip of the tea. "East Boston. Nowhere else."

"Maybe she lives in East Boston."

"Still?"

"Wouldn't surprise me. My mom's lived there for," he paused to think, "I don't even know how long."

Bizzy was doing the math in her head. "Thirty years."

"Wow."

"You came over when you were ten, right? She never moved from East Boston."

"Right. Some people don't move." He was looking over her shoulder now. "How old would Angela be now?"

They both looked at the screen full of lists. "Probably 60 or around that."

She clicked on names. "This says she lives on Highland." She made the screen bigger. "It looks like she had several names."

"Aliases. Maybe? Where are you looking?" He grimaced and went back into the kitchen. "Tea is *not* for me." He dumped the tea and was back at the counter with the little cup, pressing the button on the espresso machine again. It had its own unique gurgle, a deeper sound. It made sure you knew it was an espresso machine. *Every appliance has its own personality.*

"One of those online white pages things. Your buddy Joey Montini at *Terminal M* said she was married several times. I see a lot of these names goes back to Gotti."

She clicked on the link. And the phone number was on the screen. She pulled her phone closer to her. He put his hand over hers on the phone.

"What are you going to say?"

"Hi, my name is Bizzy Devlin. Did you work at the Pullen Pointe County jail back in the late eighties, early nineties?"

"I'd hang up."

"Then I'll call her back."

He groaned. "Just be careful."

"You keep groaning. And you keep saying that."

"I know, but..."

"It's Edy."

He took a sip of his espresso. "You're right."

She twirled around on the counter chair. "Maybe I'll go over and ask Schaeffer. He might know for sure."

"I'm sure he'll be so helpful." He went back to his own computer, which was sitting on the couch. Luigi went to get up when he saw Bizzy headed to the door.

"You stay here this time, boy."

~

WOLF MUST HAVE BEEN in a good mood, Bizzy mused as she made her way up the back path to Schaeffer's back door. He only greeted her with barking instead of the ferocious growls from before.

Schaeffer was the one who growled. "Who's there?"

"Bizzy."

There was a pause, while she heard Schaeffer inside yelling at Wolf to stop barking and go to his bed.

"What do you want? You got Wolf all agitated."

That dog is always agitated. Just like his owner.

"Quick question." Bizzy tried to sound pleasant, but the dog's barking and Schaeffer's gruff voice made it nearly impossible.

"Whatever it is, the answer is no," came the reply from the closed door.

"Can you just open the door, please?"

After a minute she heard his footsteps coming toward the door and the smell of cigar. *Ugh, I forgot he smoked those awful things.*

It took him two tries to pull open the door this time. *Just fix the warped frame, Schaeffer.*

He stood there, unshaven, in an unbuttoned wrinkled Hawaiian shirt and khaki shorts, also unbuttoned at the top.

"What do you want?" he growled.

All of sudden she felt nervous. *Calm, stay calm.*

"I wanted to ask you about someone who used to work at the jail. She worked there when you did."

Schaeffer only gave her a blank face.

"Angela Gotti? You said she was one of the few women who worked there."

His face softened a little, and then he smiled. His smile made her even more nervous. *Please don't smile.*

"Angie. Sweet girl. Had trouble finding the right man."

"How long was she at the jail?"

"A few years."

"When Tony was there, right?"

He nodded.

"Were you friends with her?"

"Nah, not really. We just all flirted with her. She was the only broad there, really. Done?"

He went to close the door. She put her hand up.

"No, no, stay open. Was she having an affair with Tony?"

Now he started to laugh. It sounded like his growl, but with a maniacal twist.

"Cheating on Edy?"

"Yeah."

"Are you *kidding*? Edy would have killed him."

Bizzy stepped back.

"Not for real. *Maybe* for real." Schaeffer's voice quivered a little. "Nah, she was feisty but never..."

"What about Angela?"

"She seemed to be doing okay with that husband. The second or third one. She liked to flirt, too. And everyone liked to flirt with her. I mean, Fred and I used to say she could have any..."

"Have you seen her? Do you know where she lives?"

"East Boston."

"Really?"

She must have been giving off a weird face. "What's wrong with East Boston?"

"I just don't expect people to live in the same place for such a long time."

Schaeffer shook his head. "I've lived in Pullen Pointe my whole life. And here," he motioned to his house, "for 40-odd years."

"You're right."

"Heck, you've lived here a lotta years, right?"

Bizzy nodded.

"See?"

"Well, that helps."

"Plus, I saw her a couple of weeks ago in Orient Heights."

What a... "Thanks, Schaeffer." She turned around and started back to her house.

"When they gonna get back to that renovation? It might be easier if you just moved." He laughed one of his growl laughs, and Wolf barked with him.

She hardly heard the last part. Instead, she concentrated on not tripping on the rotting wood on the path out of his yard. Today she had pants she'd like to keep intact.

Once out of the yard, she changed her mind and walked to the seawall and looked out to the water, then to the right at the jutting piece of land that used to hold the Pullen Pointe County Jail. Nothing remained of the building now, but she remembered seeing it when she first arrived. In her mind it seemed to appear on the island like a mirage. A brick building that went back to 1854. *What the heck happened there?*

∾

LUIGI STOOD IN THE WINDOW, watching and waiting. He was in the same place she had left him. When she got closer and he recognized her, his body went into full-on-happiness mode. She saw his tail wagging furiously.

He was at the door when she opened it.

"Hiya, buddy. Hiya." He jumped on her. "Only been gone for a few minutes, my little boy." She attempted to sit back down at her laptop on the counter. Luigi would have no part of it and continued to jump.

"Hey, Jacko, are you here?"

"Yup, up here on the big computer."

"I'm calling Angela. Between the addresses online and Schaeffer saying he saw her at Orient Heights, I'm going to take a chance."

She picked up the phone, pulled up the screen with the numbers, and tapped a number in.

"Hello?"

Jacko came downstairs to where Bizzy was sitting.

"Voicemail."

"Ah, yeah, that new thing."

"Very funny. Schaeffer said she's in East Boston."

"That's good, right?"

She nodded as she tapped the phone.

He stood next to her. "Don't forget today we have the pet photography shoot."

"Okay, I'll make sure I get to see her tomorrow. Or later today. I'm just going to dial numbers until..." She tapped the number into the phone. "Hello, Angela Gotti? Please don't hang up. I'm not selling anything. My name is Bizzy Devlin. I'd like to talk to you about Tony Giancarlo."

CHAPTER FOURTEEN

They arrived at the studio and parked around the back. Jacko jumped out first and jogged toward the door.

"You're in a hurry," Bizzy said as she pulled out the camera bag.

"Yeah, I'm excited about today." Jacko opened the door and put a loose brick against it to keep it open.

"You think we'll have a bunch of people?" Bizzy wasn't so sure, but Jacko's idea to throw out the invitation sounded good. *I hope we get at least one, for Jacko's sake.*

"I do," Jacko responded.

Bizzy put the bag on the ground, pulled up the handle, and began rolling it to the door. *All I want is one.* "Is the client the pet or the owner?"

"It's whoever pays."

Jacko practically danced down the hallway, flicking on lights and moving light stands.

"I hope I like animals after today." She lifted the camera bag onto a table and began to unzip the bag.

"I hope so, too." He lifted up the shades on the front

door. "For Luigi's sake." He went over to the storefront window and pulled the shades up. "MAMMA MIA!"

She ran over to him. "What?"

He pointed to the street outside their front window.

People lined up along the sidewalk outside their door and all the way down the block. She pressed her face to the window, and she saw they even formed a line around Revolutionary Square. Its sole cannon provided a seat to a woman with two cats.

"Jacko, what did you say we were giving out?"

"I said in the social media blast that we would give one free 8x10 print."

"Social media? That's all."

"Yes, and I sent it out yesterday and the day before."

"I don't think there are this many people in the entire town of Pullen Pointe."

"They're aren't."

We are never...

"I know what you're thinking, but I said on the blast that it would be first-come, first-serve from 2 p.m. to 4 p.m."

She looked out at the crowd, then down at her watch. "It's only noon."

Jacko shook his head. "I guess people took the 'first-come, first-serve' part seriously."

"*Noah's Ark* couldn't fit all these animals!"

She noticed the line wound around the square and up another street from the town center. She saw a woman at a distance with an incredibly thick neck. Then she looked closer and saw why.

She cringed. *A snake, she has a snake around her neck. Why did it have to be a snake?*

～

JACKO PRINTED out several sign-in sheets to hand to clients. "Glad I did this promotion," he said as the printer spat out the paper.

An older woman dressed to the nines for 1970 stood first in line. She had two crates sitting beside her, and Bizzy hoped that they contained cats, but the crates seemed to be moving constantly.

What wouldn't stop moving like that?

The woman smiled a caffeine-stained toothy smile, with a delicate smudge of red lipstick on her front tooth. She stepped forward. Bizzy put her finger up, to indicate one moment.

"What time is it?" She ran back to her bag, and quickly put her hair up in a messy bun. She looked in the mirror and grabbed a bit of her thigh in her slim-fitting black jeans. *When are you going to disappear? Gotta run more.*

"I think this crowd is going to be like a pack of wild animals." She laughed at her own joke, but Jacko didn't.

He started moving lights. "I think the afternoon is going to be grueling, that's for sure."

"Uh oh," she said as a Pullen Pointe police car pulled up out front, lights flashing but no siren. A young police-woman got out of the car and started walking toward their front door. The lights on the police car still flashed.

Jacko looked nervous. "I hope she's not going to shut us down."

"I wish she had turned off the lights." Bizzy strode to the front door and opened it.

Bizzy recognized the police officer immediately as one of the ones she had seen the last time she was in the station.

"Hi, Officer." Bizzy hesitated not knowing her name. "I met you the other day at the station. My dog had dug up some bones. Human bones."

The officer didn't seem to recognize Bizzy, but she smiled and put out her hand. "I'm Officer Jen." Officer Jen shifted her packed utility belt a little on her trim 5'5" frame.

And I thought carrying around camera equipment was hard.

"Oh yeah, I'm not here for that," she said, moving her arm around to the throng of people. "I'm here for this. I heard you're having a big photo shoot."

Jacko stepped forward and hung his head like he was about to confess. "Yes, we are running a special. We didn't expect this many people, Officer Jen."

"We weren't sure anyone would actually come," Bizzy said, putting the camera strap around her neck.

Officer Jen's thick black hair was pulled up into a ponytail under her Pullen Pointe Police Officer ballcap, and it swished as she looked around. "Your neighbors, the other business owners, feel like it's hurting their business."

Bizzy saw someone exiting Sal's Sub Shop with a bag and then untie their dog and get back in line. "Um, I think it might be *helping*."

"How long are you going to be shooting?"

"Two hours."

Officer Jen grimaced, shaking her head. "I'm not a photographer, but are you going to be able to shoot all these people *and* their pets in two hours?"

Not even in my worst nightmare.

"We'll get through as many as we can in those two hours," Jacko said.

"Yeah." Officer Jen's deep brown eyes sparkled with humor, "I'm thinking that, if these people don't get in here with their precious fur babies, you might have a riot on your hands. I know I would." She laughed.

"I guess I better go out and tell them." Jacko went to the door.

Officer Jen put her hand up and stopped Jacko. "It might be better if it came from me."

"Thanks, Officer." Jacko wiped invisible sweat from his brow. "I was seeing my life flash before my eyes."

"I suggest you offer them the opportunity to come back." Officer Jen shook her head, put her hand on her belt and said, "People and their pets."

"Yeah, we'll have them make an appointment. A lot of times people don't follow up," Jacko said.

They saw a few more people joining the line with their pets. People chatted with each other, some laughing. The older woman right outside the door peered in the window. She held up one of her travel crates.

"Oh, there's Mrs. O'Grady." Officer Jen waved. "Not surprised she's the first in line. When you opening?"

Both Jacko and Bizzy pulled up their watches. "15 minutes." They said it in unison.

"Go give the first 12 people sheets to fill out today," Bizzy said to Jacko, "then tell the rest to pick up our cards." She handed him a stack of cards. She picked up a piece of paper and wrote: Take a card, make an appointment. We'd love to photograph your fur baby or any pet you own. Same deal as today."

Officer Jen started for the door.

"Hey, Officer Jen, have they figured out anything about Tony Giancarlo?"

Officer Jen turned back, puzzled. "Who?"

"The bones found between my house?"

"They figure the girlfriend did it."

"Edy?"

"Is that her name?"

"Edy didn't do it."

"Well, apparently, someone heard them arguing the night he went missing and remembered her saying she was going to kill him."

"You don't know her. She'd never hurt a fly, an ant, or anything."

"Yeah, well, it's my experience and that of most police that it's usually the spouse or the lover."

Bizzy looked down at the back of her camera. "Who would remember something like that 25 years later?"

"Don't know. One of the guys down the point."

"You know Schaeffer is just miserable. He'd say anything right now." Bizzy could feel her face getting red. Why would Schaeffer do this? He says one thing and then...?

"That's not the name I remember."

"Then who?" Bizzy was desperate.

Officer Jen shook her head. "Can't say. Don't remember." She opened the door and went out. They heard her as she went down the line of the crowd.

"Okay people, they are only going to photograph the first twelve people and pets in line."

A huge collective groan came from the waiting crowd.

"But you will take a card, make an appointment, and they will give you the same deal you would have gotten today."

Jacko went outside and put a little table out there with cards and other advertising material. He weighed it down with a small box. He waved to the crowd and then ran back into the studio.

"There are a few angry people out there. They are going to kill us, or have their pets do it. Maybe this wasn't such a good idea."

Who heard Edy and Tony fighting? If not Schaeffer, then who?

"Hello, Bizzy?" Jacko's voice brought her back to the present moment.

Bizzy rolled her shoulders and moved her head around. "Ready."

"People are little miffed out there."

"Let's start, Jacko." She waved Mrs. O'Grady in.

MRS. O'GRADY GAVE Jacko the sheet with her name, contact information, and the names of her pets. Jacko peered out the window. Most of the crowd had dispersed after taking cards. The people in line told anyone who joined that the spots available for the day were filled.

"Keep it to ten minutes," Jacko said before letting Mrs. O'Grady in. "Don't be a perfectionist."

Mrs. O'Grady removed her coat. "Do I look all right?"

"You look lovely. Go like this." Bizzy motioned to her to wipe her front two teeth. "Now, who is your cat?" She glanced down at the sheet and saw two names: Edward and Charles.

"Cat?"

Bizzy then saw the pets: ferrets. Mrs. O'Grady opened the crates and removed two large ferrets. Bizzy stepped back.

"My boys. Meet Edward," she held up one, and then she held up the other. "Charles."

"So Eddie and Charlie," Bizzy said, pulling the camera to her face. Through the viewfinder, Mrs. O'Grady's face showed anger.

"No, Edward and Charles. They go by their given names. No nicknames for my princes."

So glad she can't see my face behind this camera.

"Of course. Smile, Mrs. O'Grady. Those boys are handsome." Charles and Edward were constantly on the move scurrying up and around their owner, but eventually they laid for a moment on each of Mrs. O'Grady's shoulders. They seemed affectionate and nuzzled at her neck. Throughout their movements, Bizzy snapped several photos. *Okay, they are hyper, but sort of cute.*

"What are your settings?" Jacko said, their code phrase to remind her to wrap it up.

Bizzy took a close-up of the two ferrets and Mrs. O'Grady and glanced down at the back of the camera. *Really sweet.*

"Can I see?" Mrs. O'Grady stood up.

She caught Jacko's eye, and he shook his head.

"Mrs. O'Grady, we will have these shots ready in a few days. And you can see them all at once," Bizzy said.

"We will email you," said Jacko.

"Oh. I have to wait that long?"

She put Edward and Charles back in their crates, reached into her pocket and pulled out treats, and fed each ferret. They gobbled them up. She put her coat on. She applied another coat of lipstick and smacked her lips.

"Thanks for coming by with Edward and Charles."

She left, smiling, with another swatch of lipstick on her front teeth.

"Bizzy, keep it to ten shots, ten minutes, remember?"

"I'm trying. Those ferrets were just so -"

He stared at her.

"Ten minutes, ten shots."

~

BY THE TIME they reached the eighth person and pet, they had seen a slew of furry, feathery, and scaly pets. One young man with spiked hair named Tim had brought his gecko named Greg. Tim kept asking Bizzy to pet Greg so that the gecko would smile. The fifth or sixth time Bizzy stroked the gecko, Tim said Greg was smiling. Bizzy couldn't tell the difference between smiling Greg and unsmiling Greg. But his skin changed color slightly as she stroked him.

When ten-year-old Shelly walked in with her pet gold-fish Delilah, Bizzy started laughing. Tears came to Shelly's eyes.

"No, no, I'm so grateful you have that cute goldfish in its bowl."

Shelly and Delilah stared at her. Bizzy knew at once that Shelly was older than her years. Her long blond hair was a little below her shoulders, and she wore a headband that matched the ribbon tied around the opening of the goldfish bowl.

"Shelly, is your mother with you?" Jacko asked, also trying to stifle a laugh.

"She's at Thomasina's."

"Thomasina's?" Jacko asked.

"Around the corner, the stylist up on Stucco Street." Bizzy motioned with her head to the left.

"Oh." Jacko reached for Shelly's sheet.

"Mommy is getting her nails done." She handed Jacko her client sheet. "She signed it. She said if you need to see her that she'll wave to you when you go by."

"I believe you," Bizzy said as Jacko walked out the door to the right.

"He's going the wrong way," Shelly said.

"Yup, he'll figure it out."

Shelly took a folded up piece of paper out of the little backpack that served as her purse. "Here's what I'm thinking." She handed Bizzy a magazine photo portraying a girl roughly Shelly's age with her gold fish.

"Is this the photo you want?"

Shelly nodded.

"Then this is what we will do." She put the magazine photo on the table. "Okay, let's find a stand we can put the fish bowl on."

"It's Delilah's room."

"Right."

They both saw Jacko trot past the studio window.

"I guess he figured it out," Shelly giggled.

Bizzy put a small table in front of the white backdrop. She then put a plain black velvet cloth over the table. Shelly set Delilah on the table.

"Okay, let's take some test shots."

Shelly nodded and placed her face behind the fish bowl. Shelly's eye looked big in the bowl, but Delilah swam toward her. "I love you, Delilah."

Please let that fish live a long life. That kid will be devastated...

Jacko came back into the studio. "Saw your mom, Shelly."

"Is she almost finished?"

"I don't know. She sat at a table holding her hand under a little fan."

"Perfect timing. We're finished, too."

"You only want that one shot?"

"You took several. I heard the clicks."

"I did. You want to see?"

Shelly came over, and Bizzy lowered the camera. The little girl smiled wide. "I love it. You got our matching hair ribbons. Thank you, Ms. Devlin." Shelly held out her hand.

"You can call me Bizzy."

"Not allowed to call an adult by their first name."

"Okay, Miss Shelly. It was a pleasure." She took Shelly's hand.

Shelly went over to Jacko and shook his hand. "Thank you, Mr. Rossi."

Shelly made sure her backpack was in the right spot on her back and walked out with Delilah.

When the door closed, Bizzy giggled. "Cute girl. Please, God, don't let her have to flush that fish for a really long time."

"Her mom said that was her fifth gold fish in the last two years."

"Okay," Bizzy said, changing cards in the camera. "She's used to the pain."

"Guess what? We only have one more."

"Really?"

"Nine, 10 and 11 couldn't wait, so they took cards and will call for appointments."

"Sweet, 'cause this two-hour session is going on two-and-half hours now."

"And whose fault is that?" Jacko went to the door. "Come on in."

Kevin Brewster, a very tall, very big man in his late 60s walked in with one of the biggest dogs she'd ever seen. The owner and pet matched in an odd way.

"This is my dog, Apollo. I had made an appointment, but -"

"Oh, so it was *you*. We couldn't make out your name on

the voicemail." Bizzy said, looking over at Jacko. "What kind of dog?"

"Bullmastiff."

"Big," Bizzy said, motioning for both Kevin and Apollo to move to the white backdrop. She noticed that they hardly fit within the backdrop. "Jacko, can you pull the bench over for Kevin to sit on?" Jacko gave her a look. "Kevin is going to sit on it, not the dog."

He pulled the bench over, and Kevin, the human, sat on it. "Can you have Apollo sit right next to you?"

They look alike.

"Smile."

Jacko snapped his fingers next to the camera to get the dog's attention. Apollo turned toward the camera, and Bizzy snapped away.

"What are your settings?" Jacko asked for the umpteenth time that day. She scanned the back of her camera.

"They're good. I think we're done, Kevin." The dog turned toward her. "And you too, sweety." Apollo the dog began to shake his head.

"No, Apollo," the human stood up. "Cover your camera!" Bizzy turned around and put the camera under her shirt. She felt something wet hit her back.

"Oh my!" Jacko said.

When she turned around, she saw that dog drool had splattered around the room.

"I'm so sorry. Do you have a rag? A paper towel?" Kevin ran around wiping up drool.

"It's okay, Kevin and Apollo. No harm to the camera."

"I think we need to do an outside shoot. I wanted to bring his sister, but I figured it would be too much."

Too much? And Apollo is just right?

"We'd love to do an outside shoot," Jacko said as he wiped up some more. "Want to do a beach shot?"

"Can I bring Lily?"

"Of course," Bizzy found herself saying. "What's one more?"

～

AFTER THEY FINISHED CLEANING UP, they turned off the studio lights and placed the cameras in their cases. Jacko plopped onto the studio couch. "So, Bizzy of Bizzy Devlin Photography, do you want to do pet photography?"

Bizzy nodded. "It was fun."

"Really?"

"Yeah, really. The more important question is," Bizzy zipped up the camera bag and stood it upright ready to roll out the door, "who said that Edy threatened Tony the night he went missing?"

Jacko fell back on the couch and groaned.

CHAPTER FIFTEEN

Angela Gotti, now Angela Jenkins, sat down at Deb's Diner smack in the middle of Pullen Pointe Center. Angela had told Bizzy she could meet her at the diner around 10:30 a.m. Bizzy had no trouble finding Angela, since she was sitting in what Bizzy considered "her booth" when she arrived. Deb had probably directed her there.

"My family has a bunch of multi-family houses, and I live in the one where I grew up," she said as she combed her long, well-manicured nails through her very grey hair. She had a cool white streak in the middle of her head. She looked exotic and sexy at 66 years old. Sixty-six, that's what the Internet had said, but sitting in front of her, she looked a bit older. The Internet gave her enough information to find Angela's phone number. The house still had a landline, which surprised Bizzy, and Angela had picked up.

"Who does that?" Bizzy had asked Jacko.

"People who want phone calls, I guess," said Jacko. "You're the only one I know who never answers their phone."

Bizzy nodded at Angela, smiled, and then checked her phone to make sure it was on silent mode.

Deb sailed around her diner and came up to the booth where Bizzy and Angela were seated.

"The usual, Biz?" Deb asked.

"Thanks, Deb. That would be perfect."

"Coming up!" Deb headed for the kitchen.

"How can I help you, Bizzy Devlin?" Angela asked, just as Bizzy sat down.

Straight to the point. Good.

"I want to ask you about Tony Giancarlo." Bizzy noticed that Angela had a coffee and muffin in front of her.

"Okay, go ahead." She broke a small piece of muffin off. "What do you want to know about Tony?" She placed the bit of muffin in her mouth after she had asked the question.

"You know that his," Bizzy stopped and considered how she should phrase it, "his remains were found."

"I heard. Wondered what had happened to him." She had a strong Boston accent, and somehow she pulled off the smallest piece of muffin imaginable.

"What was he like?" Bizzy asked. Deb delivered her coffee. She pulled the cup close and poured a healthy portion of cream, then went for the sugar. Bizzy opened four packets of sugar to start with and added them in.

Angela stared at her. "You like your sugar."

"That might have been a tad too much," she said as she tasted it. "Nope, it's fine."

"He was a nice guy."

"You worked at the jail, right?"

"Can I ask you something Bizzy?" Angela interrupted. "Why you butting into something that's none of your business?"

"The guy was uncovered about a foot from my property. My best friend, Edy-"

"Edy?" Her face lit up.

"Did you know her?"

"Yeah. No." She pulled off another piece of muffin and put it in her mouth.

"Which is it?" asked Bizzy, puzzled.

She finished chewing her piece of muffin. "Well I knew *of* her...from Tony. But I never met her."

"Oh, so Tony spoke about her. Was it good?"

This time Angela smiled wide. A real, lipstick-and-muffin-stuck-on-her-teeth kind of smile. "That man was head-over-heels in love with Edy and didn't care who knew it."

"He said that to you?" Bizzy looked taken aback.

"Why wouldn't he?" Angela's eyes flashed with a thought. "Did you think something was going on between me and Tony? Nah. Didn't happen. I actually liked my second husband at the time." She started coughing and laughing at the same time. "And, at first, I thought Tony might be gay, because he kept on referring to Edy as 'Ed'. But that misunderstanding got ironed out."

"So did everyone know about Tony and Edy?"

"Everyone knew Tony had someone special. I knew it was Edy."

"Funny," Bizzy nodded. "I think Edy was worried something might be going on between you two."

"Why would she think that?"

"You called the house and left messages for Tony on the answering machine. And Edy thought..."

"Nope. Nothing ever happened. Never even a thought of anything happening. Period. End of story." She moved her half-eaten muffin on the plate. "I hope to God she never thought that Tony was cheating on her."

"Pretty sure she did," Bizzy whispered.

"You tell her from me, that man loved her with all his heart."

"What was going on at the jail then? Schaeffer said that Tony was a bad guard. He was doing things-"

"Ask him what *he* was doing. Or if not him, then others."

"Schaeffer?"

"Him or maybe some others. Fred Long, John Walsh..." She leaned in and lowered her voice. "There *was* stuff going on, Bizzy. Tony was helping the warden get to the bottom of it. And I thought he disappeared, because he got found out and was scared. It breaks my heart that he was murdered."

"What was going on?"

"There were guards bringing in stuff they shouldn't and selling it. Cigarettes, candy, marijuana. Evidently there was money in it. But Tony wasn't one of the ones selling."

"So why were you calling Tony at home?"

"I was calling him for Mr. Tuttle, the warden. He was trying to get to the bottom of it without bringing in the state. If the state came in, it would have been worse. So the warden asked *me* to call instead of calling himself."

"Why did people think Tony went missing?"

"Everyone thought he had been found out and fled." Now Angela had tears in her eyes. "That's what I had hoped, and the warden had hoped."

"Did you consider that he could be dead?"

"In my heart I hoped he was alive. But deep down I didn't believe he would have left Edy. Bizzy, I've lived my whole life in East Boston. And I know stuff like this can happen."

"The police think that maybe Edy had something to do with it."

She leaned backward, surprised. "Are you kidding? Why?"

"The police think Edy suspected Tony of having an affair and that she killed him in a moment of passion."

"How was he killed?"

"Looks like blunt force to the head."

"I don't know Edy. In fact, everything I know about her is from the mouth of a man who loved her deeply. Who was willing to go against everybody to be with her."

"Edy never got over it, Angela. She thought Tony left her. It broke her heart. She never tried to find anyone new. She raised her son, and that was it. And..."

"And she thought that he ran away with Angela?" She asked, referring to herself in the third person. "Tell her for me what happened, and that Tony would have never left her. Never."

Angela pulled a tissue from a big purse and dabbed her eyes.

"Thanks, Angela." Bizzy picked up her cup. "Have you spoken to the police? Or have they reached out to you?"

Angela leapt up and made her way to the door. She then came back and put a five-dollar bill on the table. "I've gotta go. I have an appointment. You be careful, Bizzy. I understand wanting to help your friend. I just don't know if dangerous people are still out there. Whoever it was that got Tony killed."

"Like who?"

"Check with Donny."

"Donny Smith, the jailbird?"

"Yup. Check with him. He might know something."

CHAPTER SIXTEEN

Bizzy rushed into her house. Jacko sat at the counter, his face peering at the monitor. She stood there, breathing heavy.

He twisted around from the counter and asked, "What happened?"

She stood there trying to form words. "I'm going to take the dog for a walk."

"I just took him out," Jacko said.

"He's my cover."

"Bizzy..."

She lifted the leash off its hook, and the dog started to get excited.

"Now what are you doing?"

"I'm going to walk the dog around the neighborhood and see if any neighbors are out." She clipped the leash onto Luigi's collar.

"What for?"

I need to nose around the neighborhood, Jacko. Schaeffer or Long have to know something.

"I'm going to ask some questions of some former jail guards. Want to come?"

"No, I'm trying to get through today's photos. I'm going to pick five, then you have to pick the final three. That way, they'll be mad at you if they don't like the selection. Also, I need to work on the social media stuff."

"Sounds good. Can you keep it to just Pullen Pointe? Some of those people came from New Hampshire."

"What we need is some kid who wants to make a few bucks doing social media stuff."

"When I get back, I'll help. We'll find somebody," Bizzy promised.

"The problem isn't *finding* one. The problem is *keeping* one."

Luigi scratched at the door and hit the bells hanging from the doorknob.

"Gotta go."

They had only walked a few feet when Bizzy turned and went up to the seawall. They climbed the three wooden steps to the wall, which was about two-and-a-half feet wide. Bizzy and Luigi walked along the top of the seawall and past several of the sea cottages, including Schaeffer's. She could hear Wolf barking and growling, even though they were a good distance away from the front of Schaeffer's house.

Hah! Going to come and get us, Wolf? The growling and barking grew fiercer. *On second thought, scratch that idea.*

Long's house came up a short way after Schaeffer's. There were only two small cottages between them. Schaeffer lived on the beachfront. But Long's house was nestled behind another beachfront cottage. It still had an ocean view, but it was partially obstructed by the Song family house in front of it. Schaeffer owned all these cottages, including Long's.

Bizzy saw Fred outside in his garden. He pushed a wheelbarrow across the small landscape. He was planting some bulbs, but Bizzy wasn't sure what kind. She got off the wall at the next set of stairs. Luigi went over and sniffed everything.

"You know you're just smelling all the usual suspects," she said out loud to her puppy. *Oh, I hope no one heard that.* She glanced around at the houses. Even though they looked quiet, she knew this was a neighborhood that had eyes - and ears. "Listen, all the dogs pee right there," she whispered to Luigi.

Fred Long saw her when he came to his gate and waved. "Bizzy."

"Hey, Fred." She waved back.

"Taking Luigi out for a stroll?"

"More like he's taking me out for a stroll."

Fred laughed. He had an easy laugh and an easy smile. Dan used to tease her about not getting stuck talking to him, or she might never escape. Dan laughed then. "He'd make your ears bleed," Bizzy remembered him saying.

Fred dumped the wheelbarrow contents into a big container, most of which was a bunch of debris.

"Cleaning up, huh, Fred?"

"Yeah, fall and spring cleanup are important. Doing fall now, of course. Also, going to plant a bunch of bulbs. Love to see those tulips coming up in the spring."

"I was wondering what you might be planting. Your garden amazes me, Fred."

"Me, too. Can't believe so many things grow here."

"Can I ask you a question, Fred? About the Pullen Pointe County Jail?"

She saw a surprised look come across his face, and then it disappeared quickly. "Sure. Don't remember much."

"How long you work there?"

"For about 30 years or so."

"Wow."

"It's a place I'd like to forget."

"Bad, huh?"

"You see a bunch of riff-raff every day. It wears on you. So when you're out, you don't want to go back. And that includes memories."

"I understand." Luigi sniffed at the wheelbarrow contents. Looked like the same mulch that had been on Edy's hostas. Edy said that Fred always had mulch and put it there.

Bizzy watched as he spread the debris evenly onto the tarp. "I will be making a trip to the town dump."

"You knew Tony, right?"

He took the rake and made it all even. What seemed to Bizzy for the tenth time.

"He was one of those guys I thought I knew. But I guess I didn't."

"What does that mean?"

"I told you, Bizzy, I don't want to go back."

"Did the police ask you —"

"Yes, they did."

He raked in the debris around again in a pile.

"Wow, the town makes you do that?"

"I don't want anything in there that might hurt somebody."

"You're so sweet, Fred." She backed away a little. "Fred, was there something strange going on at the prison?"

Fred looked over to Schaeffer's house. "No."

Bizzy noticed where his gaze went. "Was Schaeffer involved in some not-so-legal stuff?"

"Long time ago, Bizzy. I don't remember much."

Luigi moved over to the dirt to smell it. Fred put the rake up, twirling it in front of him to ward him off.

"Ewww. Careful. Don't hurt Luigi," Bizzy said.

Fred smiled back at her. "I wouldn't hurt him. Why'd you say that?"

"No reason, Fred. Just..."

He leaned the rake up against the fence. "I gotta go now. Want to finish today and get all this," he pointed to the pile, "to the dump."

"I love the way your garden looks." She pulled Luigi toward her. "Heel." The pup looked up at her, and she whispered down to him. "Just stay close."

BIZZY CLIMBED BACK on the wall with Luigi and took her phone out. She walked down the ramp to the water's edge. Luigi tugged on his leash to chase a family of gulls feasting what the waves had brought in.

Bizzy dialed Doug Williams' phone. She pulled Luigi back as she held the phone to her ear. "Doug, when you asked Fred Long questions - ".

Doug cut her off. "I didn't ask him anything. Detective Martin questioned him." Doug sounded distracted, and she could hear in the background a man asking him questions, but couldn't make out either the questions or answers.

"He told me he didn't remember anything," Bizzy said. "Wouldn't answer any questions, especially about any of the other guards at the jail. He didn't want to talk about it."

"Maybe he doesn't remember anything. You're asking

about a murder, Biz, that didn't become a murder until a couple of days ago." *Not mad at me yet, calling me 'Biz.'*

"I don't know. You're right. Bert Schaeffer seems to have a lot to say about Edy, huh?"

Again Bizzy waited while she heard Doug answer someone's questions. "Doug, are you there?"

"Bizzyyyyy."

Okay, now he's mad.

Doug continued. "How do you know what Schaeffer said or didn't say? Stop asking questions. Please, this is a murder investigation. Let *us* ask the questions. We don't know if the murderer is still out there. And you need to stay out of it. I don't want to talk about this anymore." His voice sounded tense, as well as icy, to Bizzy.

She sucked in a breath. "Are we done?"

She heard him sigh.

"Yes, we're done."

Bizzy hung up the phone. She wanted to kick something.

CHAPTER SEVENTEEN

Right after her conversation with Doug, Bizzy had called Howie the contractor. He said he'd call the next day and lay out the new schedule. "Is this how you put me off?" she asked him, miffed.

"Listen, go to any home place you like and pick out your appliances and cabinets, so you'll have that part done." She could tell he was distracted.

"Okay. I already know what I want."

"Good. Get everything ordered. And if I don't call you, call me."

Count on it. She hung up and went to her computer upstairs. There she opened her renovation file. Bizzy really *did* know what she wanted. She printed everything out and then told Jacko she'd be back in an hour or so. She headed out to drop off her order.

When Bizzy got back to the house, she looked for Jacko. She went upstairs, and, from the window, saw Jacko on the beach throwing the ball for Luigi. With each ball thrown, Luigi ran full throttle, trying to reach the ball while it was still in motion. Bizzy smiled. Her phone buzzed. A smiley photo came on the screen, and over the top it said "MOM!"

She didn't take the call or hit decline. She just turned the phone over. "Sorry, Mom, I'll get back to you."

She went into the spare bedroom where Jacko slept. Her desktop computer was set up there. She sat down and turned it on. It took a little while for it to boot up. When it did, she opened a browser and typed "Donald Smith, Quincy, MA.". Up came three Donald Smiths in Quincy. Then she typed "plumber." That narrowed it down to just one. She was looking at his website when Luigi came up to her and tried to get her to pet him. Jacko was right behind.

"Sorry, I'm looking up something on my computer," she said without turning around.

"Nope, it's your house. "

"Thanks. I found him. I think."

Jacko took off his light jacket and hung it on the doorknob. And then he went into the bathroom a few feet from the bedroom/office. He turned on the water. "Who?"

"Who?" she asked back.

"Yes, who? Who did you find?" Jacko came back into the room and found a towel on the bed to dry his hands.

"Donny Smith."

Jacko shook his head. "Who's that?"

"A frequent-flyer jailbird."

Jacko put the towel back on the bed. "Bizzy, you're way ahead of me in this conversation."

"Donny Smith was a frequent visitor to the jail but was released in the mid-90s, and then he trained to be a plumber. Now he owns his own company."

"How does this relate to Tony?"

"I'm not entirely sure, but somehow he knew Tony. I

need to find out their connection. People keep mentioning him. Angela mentioned him. Told me to ask him."

"Do the police know?"

She shrugged. "They have access to databases and all sorts of things that I don't have. They must know something."

"Then let them do it."

"Except, they *don't* seem to be doing it. I'm betting he knows what happened in that jail and possibly why Tony was killed." At this point Bizzy stood up. "Will you go with me?"

"You want me to *go* with you?"

She went back and forth in the small room, mouthing the words without speaking. "I need help," she finally said.

"And you want me to go to Quincy?"

"Yes. When was the last time you went to Quincy?"

Jacko shook his head. "I've never had a reason to go."

"Well it's time we went."

"Listen, what if Donny gets mad that you're asking him questions? What if he's the reason Tony's dead?"

"You think he could have done it?" Bizzy shrugged.

"I have no idea, Bizzy. Which is why I'd like to let the police handle it."

"We'll go and figure out if he's the right guy. Then tell Doug."

Luigi did his normal downward dog stretch, then let out a whine that sounded a lot like Chewbacca.

"I guess this little guy is telling us he needs to go out and do his business again," Jacko said. "I'll take him."

After Jacko and Luigi came back, Jacko picked up on the conversation right where he left it off.

"You're going to go right up to Donny and say, 'Hey you were in jail, right? And do you remember anything going on? Do you remember Tony the Guard? You didn't happen to kill him, did you?"

"Yeah, I was kind of going down that route, but a tad more subtle." She purposely avoided looking at Jacko's face. "Look, Donny's name has come up more than once. I want to get the reformed prisoner's point of view of what was happening at the jail, while Tony was there. And if Tony was a good or bad guard."

"And maybe he'll kill you, because you've uncovered something that he wants to stay covered."

"Maybe. Or he finally got his life together. Now he's a successful plumber. Owns his own business. He's a success story. According to Google, he's won awards."

Jacko didn't move.

"Or he could try to kill me, which is why I want you to go along."

~

BIZZY HATED TO DO IT, but Edy wasn't around to puppy-sit Luigi, so she put her little guy into his kennel. "Just to make sure that you don't get into any trouble. 'Cause you *can* be a little mischievous." Luigi flopped down in the crate and peered through the mesh with sad eyes.

"Please don't look at me like that."

"Yeah, he did chew my slipper. He still has some of his puppy 'shark teeth'".

"In his defense, he only chewed one. And they can chew at any time." She put her hand up against the crate. "That's why you're going to stay in your room."

"You think he doesn't know it's his crate?" Jacko asked as he grabbed his jacket.

Bizzy shushed Jacko. "We will be back in a flash. You

just took him out for a run a while ago. He'll sleep the whole time."

As they walked out the door and saw Luigi through the windows, he was whining and barking at his humans. "I hate seeing the little guy in there," Jacko said.

"Way to make me feel guilty." They walked down the boardwalk toward the street and Bizzy's car.

"Well, he's just so cute."

"The cutie could get into something and hurt himself. He's still too young." Bizzy walked over to her Honda CR-V driver's side and hesitated. "I'm going to have to go through the tunnel and down the expressway. It's crazy. There's so much traffic to the South Shore. People will cut me off." The panic started for her. It began in her stomach usually, then travelled up to her lungs. Then she'd have to do all the breathing exercises to calm down.

"You can do this," Jacko said softly. "I tell you what, you drive there. I'll drive back. And if you really need to switch drivers, say the word and we can swap out."

"Deal." She walked to the door and opened it.

"Did you even lock the door on this thing?"

She hit the fob, and then hit it again. "I did. It's silent."

They both got in the car. She put her phone in its holder. She already had the address punched in, so she pressed "Go" on the GPS. The directions came on with a man's voice in a British accent.

"Your Siri is an Englishman?"

"I like it. It feels very Downton Abbey to me. And his name isn't Siri for me. He prefers to be called Nigel."

"Oh my, Bizzy."

She knew he was rolling his eyes. She heard them go into the back of his head.

It was nearly 3 p.m., so rush hour would be starting

soon. Nigel told her to take a left onto Main Street, and they made their way down Saratoga to Bennington. She made a left.

"Why are you going that way?"

"Listen you, I will pull over if you even try to tell me how to drive or which way to go. I listen to Nigel."

"Nigel should have told you to go straight up to 1A."

Now she turned to him. "I trust Nigel. Do I ever say anything to you when you drive?"

"All the time, Bizzy. All. The. Time. You say I drive like a crazy Italian. And frankly, I do. But that's because I learned to drive in Italy. We all drive like our Fiats are actually Ferraris."

They remained silent, and, as luck would have it, Boston traffic was only slightly congested on the way to Quincy. They went through the Ted Williams Tunnel and were dumped onto 93 South. Jacko held on to what they called the vehicle's "Oh, Jesus!" handle when Nigel told her to get off at Exit 12 for Quincy. Bizzy followed Nigel's soothing voice until they arrived at Smith Plumbing.

She pulled over and parked. "You're safe now."

Jacko let go of the handle and wiped his hands on his pants.

The place had no cars in front of the building and appeared desolate. *What if no one's there?*

"Is this the right place? They have to come back to the office, right? Isn't that what plumbers do?"

"I don't know." Jacko twisted his head, searching the street for signs of life. Other nearby businesses had the same desolate appearance. "They'd all be leaving jobs now, I think."

The establishments had electrician and HVAC signs on them.

"They probably have a secretary or office manager." Bizzy pressed her face against the car window.

They waited. At 3:45 the street started to hop, as vans drove down the street going to the different businesses. One van pulled up to the building that held Smith Plumbing, and then a second. A young plumber opened the door and circled around the back of the van. He grabbed a bunch of papers and walked into the office. He was tall and lanky with a Red Sox cap on. On the back of his shirt, it said "Smith Plumbing."

"Okay. Let's go." Bizzy hopped out of the car.

"Okay, Nancy Drew, I'm following your lead."

They both walked across the street, toward Smith Plumbing.

When they opened the door, a bell rang, announcing their entrance, and they walked into the office. The young plumber who had just entered stood next to a desk talking to a sixtyish woman. She was casually dressed with a red polo shirt that said "Smith Plumbing" across one side of her chest. Her dark hair had slivers of gray, and it was pulled back into a tight bun. She wore her glasses on the tip of her nose and peered over some paperwork on her desk.

"Can I help you two?"

The young man smiled at both of them.

Bizzy glanced around.

"Hey, can I *help* you?" the woman asked again.

"Oh yeah, yeah." Bizzy stood there a moment. *Not sure what to say.*

"Is Donny Smith available?"

The woman's eyes narrowed. "Who wants to know?"

"Bizzy Devlin and," she looked over to Jacko, "Giacomo Rossi."

"He's in his office," said the young man.

As soon as he said the words, the woman slapped his arm. "You don't know who these people are. Your father probably doesn't know them."

He recoiled. "Mom, don't do that." The young man shrugged and walked away.

"I'll see if he's available," the gray-haired woman said and walked back to the office. They followed her.

～

DONNY SMITH WAS A SLIGHTLY rotund guy, but still had a full head of reddish gray hair. She imagined him in tight, cramped places where plumbing was needed and hoped he didn't get stuck. The thought almost made her laugh.

"Hello, Donny." Bizzy put out her hand, but Donny didn't take it. He showed her his dirty, blackened hands.

"You don't want to shake these hands. I can never really get the dirt and grime off."

Bizzy smiled. Jacko stiffened beside her.

"Donny, could we speak to you in private? I promise it won't take much time."

"Sure, go ahead. It's private here."

"Ahem." The woman who had shown them in still remained at the door.

Donny put his hands down. "It's okay, Bev." He smiled at the woman. "Bev's my better half, *and* the business manager, *and* fantastic mother of Donny, Jr., who just came in from a tough job."

Bev gave Bizzy the side eye but then left the office. She pushed the door so it remained wide open.

Pipes and papers in equal parts lay strewn all over, and plenty of dirt covered the floor. On a table, a pipe structure resembled a piece of modern art, and Bizzy wanted to know what it was.

"What can I help you with?" he asked, wiping his hands on a rag.

"Well, I wanted to ask you about a guy named Tony Giancarlo."

Bizzy observed him: He didn't blink, and the smile stayed on his face.

"Good guy. He was one of the guards at the Pullen Pointe Jail. You are?"

"Bizzy Devlin. My best friend, Edy Tyne, was Tony Giancarlo's sweetheart."

"Ah. Tony's girl. I remember. Man, he loved that woman. Almost as much as I love my Bev."

"Yes, she was his girl." Bizzy hesitated. She didn't have any idea if the police had spoken to Donny.

"The police found him buried on her property, right?" Donny finally asked.

"*Between* our properties. May I ask what you were in the jail for?" Bizzy thought she would cut to the chase.

"Something stupid. In my misguided youth," he shook his head but still had the smile on his face, "I did some burglary, more than once. Got caught. Luckily, I wasn't quite dumb enough to carry a weapon. The first couple times I went to Pullen Pointe Jail, which is where I met Tony. But after the third conviction, they made me do a little hard time to reinforce that stealing was not a good career choice. Tony encouraged me to do something different with my life. He helped me get some training as a plumber, and here I am. Not proud of my past, but it made me change and become a better person today. And I got Bev and Donny, Jr. here. Life is good. Lucky me."

"Yeah, lucky. Did Tony treat you well?"

"He treated *everyone* fair. It didn't always bode well for him, though. With the other guards."

Jacko fidgeted. And Bizzy noticed he now stood at the doorway, leaning up against the door.

"Yeah. Some of the guards had their own thing going." He laughed. "Some of them should have been wearing the uniform *I* was wearing." He laughed at his joke.

"How's that?" Jacko asked.

"They were helping some of the guys get hard-to-find stuff. That stuff was tame compared to what's going on now."

"Were you one of those guys?"

"Me? No. I didn't smoke cigarettes or joints. And I didn't do 'special visits' with the ladies. To be honest, I spent my time in there reading about how I could become a plumber." He smiled. Bizzy smiled back.

"So was Tony one of those guards?"

Donny nodded. "I didn't figure Tony to be part of anything. He asked me one time if I knew anything about the contraband. I told him I knew a little, but was keeping my nose out of other people's business. Like I said, he was a nice guy. And he helped me."

Jacko spoke up. "Well, what guards were involved? Did the police ask you?"

"No. All they asked was if I knew him. And I did. You're not the police, right?"

"No," Bizzy said. "I'm just a friend of a lady who loved Tony."

Jacko squirmed a little and shifted his weight from one foot to the other and back again. "We are not police."

Ugh, Jacko why'd you say it that way?

"Listen, we are just are trying to find out for our friend."

She rushed the last bit. "Did Tony ever talk about Edy? Any problems?"

Donnie stopped for a minute and smiled. "He talked about her. In love. She was feisty, with a little bit of a temper sometimes."

"That's Edy," Bizzy replied. "But she's mellowed now. Did you know if he might have been seeing another woman? Angela?"

Donny shook his head. "No way. Not Tony. Angela was the warden's secretary. And she did like men, but I never heard that she and Tony had anything going on. Besides, the way he loved Edy, I wouldn't have believed it if I heard it."

"So you're convinced Tony wasn't doing anything illegal." Bizzy said.

"I told you, not that I knew of." He didn't look at her. His smile had now disappeared.

"It's so long ago, Donny. Everything is past. This is about someone's innocence, and her heart."

Bev stood at the door. Donny looked at his wife standing in the doorway. Her arms were firmly folded in front of her. "There was stuff going on. But Tony wasn't the one doing it."

"Did you think something was strange when Tony didn't show up?"

"I just thought he quit. High turnover there. Some of the other guards were just mean, difficult. With the prisoners and with each other." He shook his head.

"The guards were mean?"

"There were a couple. Not Tony. But there were a couple."

"Like who?" Bizzy pushed.

"I don't really remember. There were a few."

"What about a guy named Schaeffer?" Jacko asked the question, and Bizzy turned around to him.

"Schaeffer was an ornery human being."

"That doesn't surprise me," Bizzy said.

"You know him?" asked Donny.

"He worked at the jail a long time, and he is my neighbor. It must have been a bummer when he had to go to the South Shore to the new jail."

"Don't think he went."

"No?"

"No, doll, I don't think so. I remember the guards that went. And he wasn't there."

"Why?" Bizzy asked.

"Bizzy, I wouldn't know why people make the choices they do."

"No rumors. Or *anything*?"

His head went back and forth. "Well, there was some talky talk, not even really rumors."

"What kind of talk was there?" Jacko interjected the question. Bizzy almost smiled. He was starting to get in to the interrogation.

"There is always talk. Always rumors. You never know what's true or not."

"But you remember something?"

"Schaeffer, I thought, had to resign. Well, that's what someone said. The warden made him resign."

"Anybody know why?"

"Not me. There was another guy who didn't go to the new jail, either. He wasn't mean, but he wasn't exactly everyone's favorite. I want to say his last name was Long."

"Fred Long?"

"You know him, too?"

"Also a neighbor."

"Dang, this does not sound like a great place to live."

"Actually, it is," Bizzy said. "I knew about Schaeffer, but not about Long. I thought he went."

"Maybe it was him who had to resign. Nah, pretty sure it was good ol' Schaeffer. Law and order guy."

CHAPTER EIGHTEEN

Two hours later, after braving rush hour traffic back to Pullen Point, Bizzy plopped onto the couch. She listened to a terse voicemail message Doug had left.

"Bizzy Devlin, I'm on my way over to see you, so *be home.*"

Oh yeah, he is annoyed.

Jacko saw her face as she listened to the message. "What's up?"

"Doug is on his way over."

He looked around the house, which was a mess from packing and moving stuff for the renovations. The place had an after-the-hurricane-carnage look.

"We don't need to clean up, do we?"

Jacko had a streak of neat freak in him.

"I'm not going to. And *you* are not, either."

A particular thud on the boardwalk, a heavy-footed stomp, caused Luigi run to the window to investigate. *Here he comes.* When the bang on the door finally came, Luigi scurried to the door. Doug walked in, and Bizzy almost laughed. He looked a little like a blowfish. And his windbreaker was wrapped around his body in an odd way, like he had put it on in a hurry.

"Hey, Doug, come on in." Luigi ran to him and jumped up and down. "Down, Luigi. Down! Sorry about that, Doug."

Luigi went over to Jacko, who was putting on a jacket.

"I'll take you for a walk in little while," Bizzy said.

Don't you dare leave, Jacko.

"I have to leave. I promised I'd take Mama to Medford. I left some stuff for salad on the counter, and I should be back in a bit."

She tried to send him a message through her eyes, but he didn't look back as he left.

Are you purposely ignoring me, Jacko?

Jacko walked out the door.

She sighed, then glanced over to the counter full of veggies for salad. She started chopping the veggies that Jacko had left there.

"What are you doing?" Doug asked.

She picked up the knife to show him. "Cutting veggies." She went to the cutting board and continued slicing onions.

Nope, there is no good reason for me to do this now.

"You went over and talked to Donny Smith?"

She stopped slicing but didn't turn to him. She sucked in a breath. The onions got to her. "Yeah, I did."

"Did it occur to you that you were interfering with police business?"

Now she turned to him, her face scrunched up a little, trying to hold back tears. "Interfering? No. I thought you had already questioned him."

"What do you not get here?" His face went crimson red. "How many times do I have to tell you? This is police business. Stay out of it."

"Doug, a murder was committed. Of course it is police business." Bizzy couldn't stop the tears.

Darn. He is going to think I'm crying about him yelling at me.

She grabbed a paper towel, and put it up to her eyes. Then she put it under cold water and patted the front of her face.

"Well," Doug stammered, his voice softening, "could you not interfere with police business? Do not go question people that might have vital information." He stopped talking. "Are you all right?"

She continued to dab her face. "Do you still think Edy did it?"

"She is a strong - *very* strong - person of interest."

"Well, she didn't do it."

"How do you know?"

"Because they were in love."

"Bizzy, I can give you the names of a dozen people who were murdered by their spouses or lovers. They were *all* in love."

She stared at him. "That body was not there 25 years ago. Someone put it there ten years ago when we did our deck."

"Who would have done that, Bizzy?"

"I don't know, but I'm trying to find out."

"That is *not* your job. I heard you talked to Schaeffer, too."

"Yes, I did. He's my neighbor, if you hadn't noticed. Wasn't a lot of help. And I spoke with Angela."

"Angela?" Doug lifted his eyebrows.

"The woman who left messages on Tony's machine. She worked at the jail."

"By all accounts, someone Tony was having an affair with," Doug said.

"Maybe that was the rumor. But she wasn't."

"How do you know that? Because she told you so?"

Bizzy stopped. Now she was the one who needed to control her bubbling anger. "Actually, Angela *did* tell me so. There was no affair. Angela was the secretary for the warden. A guy by the name of Joe Tuttle."

"Well, Bizzy, he's dead, so you won't need to look him up and try and talk to him."

"Thanks for the heads up. You already told me that, remember?" She tried to keep the sarcasm in check, but it had just leaked.

"Bizzy, stay out of this investigation."

"You know that something was going on with Tony and the warden. Tony was doing something *for* him. Angela said so, not Edy. All Edy knew was that Tony started working third shift, which he almost never did, and that Angela had left messages."

"You don't see how that looks, do you?"

"He was working third shift. Why would Angela lie?"

"There are a million reasons to lie. Like, if they were up to something illegal. Or if they were having an affair."

"But they were not!"

Doug stopped, and breathed in deeply. He glanced at Bizzy's computer and saw the photos on her screen she had taken when Tony's bones were found. "I could put you on the forensic photographer list," he said quietly. "You were good. You still are."

"I found the photos I took of the deck project ten years ago. It could prove the body wasn't there ten years ago. Want to see them?"

"No, Bizzy, I don't. I don't see how that will prove

anything. The storms and movement of sand could have changed things."

Doug walked toward the door. Luigi followed behind. "You better give this boy the walk you promised." He straightened out his jacket and walked out the door.

Bizzy got Luigi's leash, and clipped it to the metal loop on his collar. She opened the door and saw that Doug was checking out the side of the house, where the corpse had been found. He looked back at her. "You think that the body was moved here when Dan was building the deck?"

She nodded. "Sure of it. Don't you think we would have found Tony then?"

He got up and walked toward her. "Please don't get involved in this stuff. There are a lot of dangerous people out in the world, Bizzy Devlin. Remember that."

"How can I forget? I photographed their deeds for years."

Doug walked past her and down the boardwalk.

Bizzy walked with her dog toward the beach, but she heard coughing. Deep-lunged, smoker coughing. Over the fence she could see the top of Schaeffer's head.

She glanced back at the fence between their properties. *Were you eavesdropping, Schaeffer?*

SHE BRAKED hard when she went into the parking spot behind the studio and came within an inch of hitting the brick wall. Jacko had taken his mother grocery shopping and said he'd see her later at the house. Right after Doug left, he called.

"Bizzy, we forgot!" he yelled into the phone.

"What? Was it something to do with the murder investigation?"

"Mrs. O'Grady is waiting for us at the studio. We had an appointment with her."

"We did?"

"Yes, it's in the book at the studio and in my phone —"

"Jacko!"

"I'm in Medford at the Italian Market, and I won't get there in time. My computer..." He told her where everything was. He had whittled it down to five pictures, but then put a few extra in the folder. Now it was ten.

"Why can't we email them to her?"

"Because she doesn't check email. She has it, she says, but she doesn't use it."

Bizzy groaned loudly. More of a low growl. Luigi scurried over to his bed.

"Ha," he said, trying to shout over his mother ordering food in Italian at the Italian Market, "you sound like me."

"Is that Italian?"

"Biz, it's an Italian Market."

"In Medford?"

"Yep."

Bizzy groaned again. "I have to meet Mrs. O'Grady all by myself."

"It's *ten* photos. It will take a few minutes."

Bizzy hung up and glanced down at Luigi. "I have to go see Mrs. O'Grady at the studio. Jacko said it will only take a few minutes. You want to come?"

Luigi tilted his head to the right and to the left.

"Glad you want to come. Not sure I can handle Mrs. O'Grady all by myself."

When they arrived at the studio, Luigi hopped into the driver's seat. He stared at Bizzy.

She tugged on his leash to take him out of the car. "Come on, little guy. That seat is not yours. You can't even drive." He gave her a little yelp and jumped out of the car.

As Bizzy unlocked the studio back door, Luigi scrambled inside and ran to the front door. Then he started barking, with a small undertone of growl.

"Stop, Luigi. It's just Mrs. O'Grady."

Mrs. O'Grady had pressed her face against the window of the door. Some of her lipstick remained on the window as she pulled away and waved.

Is that Charles and Edward's crate? Oh, no.

She opened the door, and Mrs. O'Grady tumbled in the door with the boys thumping around in their crate.

"Hello, Bizzy. The boys and I are ready!" At that moment she saw Luigi on his way to investigate the soft crate in her hand. Bizzy thought, as the dog walked over to it, that the crate looked a little flimsy. She suddenly saw the scene in slow motion: Luigi jumping at Mrs. O'Grady, and the ferrets hitting the sides of their crate, clawing to get out.

"Luigi, come!"

Mrs. O'Grady dropped the soft crate carrying Edward and Charles. Luigi stood over the crate as one of them, Bizzy couldn't really tell which, escaped through a hole in the crate. Then the other one popped out.

The ferrets ran, and Luigi ran after them. What the ferrets had going for them was the ability to crawl into small places. Bizzy chased after Luigi, but every time she came close to grabbing his collar, he managed to escape and continue chasing the ferrets.

"I'm so sorry, Mrs. O'Grady," Bizzy said as she ran and got Luigi's leash. Now the ferrets and the dog were running amok. One ferret would come out of hiding and get very close to Luigi, and Luigi would run after him. Then the other would catch Luigi's attention and do the same thing.

"Charles, come to Mother." Charles glanced over at Mrs. O'Grady, then back at Luigi. And their little game started all over again. Edward crept out from under the couch. Luigi went after him but couldn't catch him. Again, the ferrets baited the dog and then ran away. Finally, Luigi caught him.

"Don't eat Edward!" Mrs. O'Grady cried.

"Luigi, come!"

Luigi, though, just leaned down and sniffed the ferret under his paw. Then he licked him. They were locked in stares, and then Charles scurried out and Luigi looked over at him. Meanwhile Edward escaped from under Luigi's paw.

"Bizzy, I think they're playing."

Bizzy saw that all three were running around, but that the ferrets had the upper hand.

"I think your boys are teasing my puppy." Bizzy laughed, but she was close enough now to grab Luigi and popped the leash on him in order to secure him.

"Don't be an overprotective mother, Bizzy. Just let them play." Mrs. O'Grady sat down on the couch that her boys considered home base for their game of 'bait the puppy.' "I'm so looking forward to seeing our portraits."

Luigi barked, clearly wanting to continue playing chase with his clever friends. But Bizzy took the leash and wrapped it around a chair leg. "It might be easier to see the photos if the big boy here sits by me."

"True. Edward and Charles were looking forward to seeing the photos, too."

Bizzy walked over to the other side of the studio. "Just let me get my computer, and-" Her phone buzzed in her pocket, but Bizzy didn't answer. She got her computer out of her backpack and opened it as she returned to Mrs. O'Grady.

The phone buzzed twice as she set the laptop on the small table in front of her client, and she opened it.

"Just a sec, Mrs. O'Grady." She pulled out her phone, which revealed that she missed two calls from Edy. Bizzy desperately wanted to call her back, but she set the laptop up to the program where the photos were.

"Mrs. O'Grady, I want you to pick two photos to print. I think you wanted one of each." The ferrets were on the couch next to their human mother, and now each one climbed up an arm and onto her shoulder.

"All you have to do is click this button," Bizzy showed her, "to go forward. And this one," she showed her the other arrow," to go back. I just need to go to the bathroom. I'll be right back." She looked over to Luigi and said, "You be a good little boy."

She hurried down the hall and grabbed her phone. Now there was a text from Edy.

The police have taken me in.

CHAPTER NINETEEN

B izzy swished around veggies in a pan. "Add a pinch of salt and a twist or two of cracked pepper, and we will have dinner."

"As much as I like to try to new things, I really do not want to try veggies and tofu." Jacko said "tofu" with complete disgust.

"It's not that bad." She swished the veggies around harder.

"Are you mad at the veggies?"

She stopped and stared at the veggies in the pot. "I'm frustrated, that's all."

"She's back home, right?" Jacko asked softly.

Bizzy nodded, dumped some brown rice in a bowl, and covered it with some of the veggie and tofu mixture.

"I'm going to take this over to Edy. She loves this."

"Glad she does," Jacko shuddered.

"She's vegan."

He shuddered again. "Oh, that's why she never eats anything I make."

Bizzy stared at him, then covered the steaming bowl of food. "I'll be right back. Feel free to have some if you want."

Luigi went to follow her out the door, but she nudged him back. "Stay here with Jacko."

In less than two minutes, she returned with the bowl of food in hand.

"She says she's not hungry," Bizzy said as she opened a drawer and pulled out a fork. She sat down on the nearby couch and started eating.

"Is Edy *somewhat* okay?" Jacko asked.

"She feels awful, Jacko." Bizzy popped a piece of tofu in her mouth. "She is the main focus of the police attention. They picked up Tony's belongings today. Who knows what they will find in there that they think will implicate Edy?"

Jacko soon joined Bizzy with a bowl of food. "Hey, this isn't that bad," he said, putting small bites in his mouth.

"It's okay." She put the bowl on the ottoman in front of her. Luigi came and sniffed the bowl and walked away.

Jacko laughed. "Luigi, don't turn your nose up at your mother's cooking." He picked her bowl and took it to the kitchen.

"It will make a good lunch," Bizzy said.

It took Jacko a few minutes to clean up and put the food in containers. He left the pan in the sink.

Bizzy was worried for her friend Edy, and her face showed it. Jacko stopped his cleaning and looked squarely at Bizzy. "You're going to prove her innocence."

"Thanks, Jacko. I'm going to do my best."

Jacko reached for Bizzy's laptop sitting on the counter, and set in front of himself. "Tomorrow we are photographing Kevin and his two dogs."

"Remind me to wear a raincoat for when Apollo decides to spread his drooly love. Bring a lot of treats." While Bizzy was cleaning the pan, she glanced over at the laptop. "Just a second. Don't close that screen out."

"Where are the photos you took during the deck being built?" Jacko asked.

She hovered over Jacko and the computer. She dried her hands on her pants, then pressed a few of the keys and brought up some photos.

"Okay, look at this. Here are the photos I took of Tony when Luigi found him." Luigi heard his name and came over, nuzzling his head against the side of Bizzy's leg. "I was just saying your name, boy. You can relax."

She pointed to the screen. "Look at this." She clicked to make the photo bigger. "See this?"

Jacko nodded. "Yeah."

She moved to another photo. She zoomed in on the screen. "See right here?"

Jacko nodded again. "I don't get your point."

"One is the same area from a photo I took ten years ago, and one is a photo I took the other day when the body turned up."

Jacko took a deep breath. "I see it, but what are you getting at?"

"What do you notice?"

He shook his head, still not getting it. "I see a water meter. I see Tony's corpse in the other, and still just the meter. In the more recent photo it's rusted."

"Look at the sand levels. We would have noticed the extra bulk of a body buried there ten years ago."

"Maybe not, Bizzy. The other day, a whole lot of digging went on. So the photos don't show the sand levels before Howie and his crew did their job, and before Luigi did his digging."

"Maybe you're right," Bizzy said. Bummer!"

"Sorry to burst your bubble."

Bizzy closed her eyes for a moment, rummaging through her memory banks. "Jacko, ten years ago, the same night after taking this photo, Dan and I took Jay to a Red Sox game."

"Where was Edy?"

"She was on duty with the airline. She had flown to the West coast. I distinctly remember she had the red eye flight and didn't return until the next morning."

"So if Edy was out of town, who took this picture?"

"Fred Long did. Now that I think of it, he was the one who gave us the Red Sox tickets for that night."

Jacko stared at the screen for a moment. "Just a second, Bizzy. This picture from ten years ago is missing the last piece of the deck. It's not complete. Do you have a picture after the last piece of deck was laid down?"

"It's in there somewhere. We wanted to wait for Edy to come back to lay down the final section of deck and take the photo of the finished project together."

"Has Doug seen these pictures?"

"I offered to show Doug the pictures, but he said they wouldn't prove Edy's innocence, and kept telling me to stay out of it."

Jacko clicked ahead to the next photo. "So this must be the picture from the next day. The deck is complete in this one."

"Right, and Edy is in it," Bizzy said. "Edy and I are holding hammers to make it look like we had worked on the deck, even though our only contribution to the job was to watch and bring lemonade to the guys."

Jacko stared at the picture. He zoomed in. "Wait a minute. Look. There's a patch of dark in this picture that wasn't in the photo from the day before. See? Between the deck and Edy's house. It's not the color of sand. What is that, dirt?"

Bizzy zoomed in and said, "You're right! That's definitely dirt." She zoomed in more. "It looks like the dirt is mixed in with some mulch. Just like the mulch that stuck on Luigi's coat when he dug up the body."

"How would the dirt and mulch have gotten there?" Jacko asked. "It wasn't in the photo from the day before. And it couldn't have been Edy. You said she wasn't in town." Jacko scrunched up his face as if he were trying to do a hard math problem. "So Tony was found in a combo of dirt and mulch... " Then the light bulb came on in his head, and his face brightened. "So he was originally buried in one place when he was killed, and was reburied here ten years ago, on the very last day you had the deck completed!"

"That has to be right!" Bizzy cried. "There had never been any dirt or mulch there before. It's only ever been sand."

"And your ten-year-old picture proves that," Jacko said. "But if you and Dan, Jay, and Edy are all in this picture, who took the photo? Fred again?"

"That time we roped Schaeffer into taking the picture. We were making a bit of a ruckus celebrating. Schaeffer had popped his head over the back fence to watch. So we put him to work."

"Okay. So it's clear the body had to have been moved to Edy's. The question remains, where was Tony buried originally?"

"That's the million-dollar question."

Jacko peered closer at the picture of Tony's bones. "Does he have something in his hand?"

Bizzy peered closer. "No, but it looks like something might have been in it. Sometimes rigor mortis sets in.

Though you may take something from the hand, the hand keeps the shape it was in when the person died."

She took a long deep breath. Jacko turned to her. "What are you thinking?"

Clicking on the photo, zooming in and out, she finally turned to Jacko. "I'm thinking we should go out in the neighborhood and look around," said Bizzy.

Jacko's hands moved before the words came out of his mouth. "You want us to go out *now*, at seven o'clock in the evening? Besides, you said you're cooking tonight."

"I *did* cook. We already had dinner."

"Tofu and veggies does not qualify for dinner."

"It's not that dark out yet." Bizzy said. "This is a really sandy neighborhood. We just go and look around at people who have dirt and mulch."

"We're literally gonna be walking through people's yards? Is that what you're thinking?" Jacko asked. "Besides, if they had dirt and mulch ten years ago, it doesn't mean they still do today."

"Possibly. But most people who do gardening seem to hold on to that bad habit for years and years. For my mother it's been a lifelong addiction."

Luigi went over and hit the strand of bells on the door. "Jacko, we are just going to take Luigi out for a walk. We could pretend like we lost him."

Jacko just looked at her, then back to the dog. "You'd sacrifice your puppy-son?" Luigi swiped at the bells again, this time with a little more urgency.

She's moaned, "You're absolutely right. I can't do that. We'll just take him on the leash and have him sniff everything. See what he comes up with. He *did* come up with the body."

"I don't know, Bizzy. Why does the killer have to be

someone around here? He could have been killed by anyone and buried anywhere." Luigi found the ball and brought it to Jacko, inviting him to play.

"At the very least," Bizzy responded, "somebody who lived in the neighborhood helped move the body to where Luigi found it. Otherwise, how would they know that we were building a new deck? Who else would know right when it was about to be finished? And what are the chances an outsider would put the body right at Edy's place, where Tony lived?"

"Good point. Someone local must have been involved."

"Exactly. Tony's body was buried once already in dirt and mulch. And then when our deck was done, or almost done, they reburied the body here, hoping that no one would ever know. Which no one ever did. Until now."

"Bizzy, it's not an easy thing to unbury and rebury a body, let alone do it without being seen. That means some-body's very determined, probably strong, and pretty clever. So we need to watch our backs."

Luigi nudged the ball into the back of Jacko's knee. "Hey boy, we're going to take you out." Luigi stuck the ball between Jacko's knees.

"And nobody ever would have known if we hadn't lifted the deck for the renovations." Bizzy went to the door. "Now we are going to find some gardens with rich, dark topsoil and mulch."

"Everyone around here who wants topsoil and mulch for a yard or garden has to bring it in, right?" Jacko asked.

"Right, Jacko. Exactly. So whoever thought this secret has been safe for ten years had a garden back then."

Bizzy and Jacko went out to where the deck had been. She looked toward the spot where the body was found. "Just gonna have to look at different yards."

Jacko pointed across the way. "There's a yard and garden."

She glanced over at the pretty seaside garden across the way. "Not Chris." Bizzy shook her head. "Chris and Bobbie would never kill anyone. No way it's Chris. They've won awards with this garden. It has to be a yard that isn't as open to public view."

"So what you're saying is they can't be the killers because their garden has won awards?" asked Jacko.

"I can't say for sure Chris didn't do it. But where's the motive? And I'm just saying this one place is a really beautiful beach garden. They've won awards. And it isn't closed in. Someone would have noticed a big hole in their garden."

"Okay. So who has gardens that are closed in, *and* you think could have killed Tony?"

They started to walk toward the beach. "You know, Fred Long has a garden. And he worked at the jail. But he's nice."

"So the nice guy can't be a murderer?" Jacko smirked.

Bizzy ignored his sarcasm. "What about Schaeffer?"

"I thought you said Schaeffer's yard was always just full of junk, stuff he collected from the beach."

Bizzy stopped. Both Jacko and Luigi, walking one step behind, bumped into her. She barely noticed the collision. "But when I went into his yard to speak to him, there was a garden against the fence in the back."

"The question is, Sherlock, did he have a garden ten years ago when the body would have been moved?"

They reached the beach wall and both turned to look at all the little cottages and beach bungalows woven together.

"On a map this neighborhood has gotta look like such a maze," Jacko said.

"Jacko, do you have Luigi's ball?" She held her hand out. Jacko didn't have it. But when Luigi heard the word "ball" he nudged Bizzy with it. She went to grab it, but he pulled away. "Drop the ball, Lou. Drop the ball." The dog came close to her. Just as Bizzy went in for the grab, Luigi backed away. This dueling match went on three times. Jacko laughed.

"He's playing keep-away, and you are definitely losing."

Bizzy stopped, reached into her pocket, and held up a treat in her hand. "Drop it." The dog eyed the object in her hand, and dropped the ball. Bizzy gave him the treat.

"That's so unfair."

"That, my friend, is why I never leave home without treats."

"Are you going to throw it?" asked Jacko. The dog was eying the ball in her hand.

"Yes, yes, I am." And then she threw it toward Schaeffer's house. It soared over the fence and into the yard. She heard Schaeffer's dog barking.

"You threw it into his yard!" Jacko said in disbelief.

Luigi was already at the fence by the time Bizzy and Jacko caught up with him. The dog was jumping at the gate. Inside the house Bizzy could hear Wolf barking, growling.

"Okay, let's go," she said, lifting the gate's latch.

"What?" Jacko gasped.

"Come on. Think of it as you being my crime-fighting partner."

"Crap, Bizzy. That is one big, loud, angry-sounding dog."

Luigi started barking now.

"Who's there?" Schaeffer called out with a snarl. It was followed by a series of coughing spasms.

Both of them froze. Neither dog barked.

The coughing stopped. "I said, who's there?"

"Hi, Mr. Schaeffer." Bizzy said it, her voice just a little too high. Air barely made it to her lungs.

"Who are you?" Schaeffer came around the corner.

"Hi, Mr. Schaeffer. I accidentally threw the ball too hard, and it went into your yard."

He was at the fence now, and he saw that they had opened the gate. "So you were just going to trespass?"

"No, no," stammered Bizzy, "I was going to knock on the door when I came in and let you know."

"Wolf could have been in the yard. That would have been your fault if he tore you to pieces."

"Yes, it would have been."

He turned to Jacko. "Who are you? Have I seen you here before?"

It took a second, but Jacko finally spoke. "Yes, you've seen me here. I'm Bizzy's assistant at the studio."

"Right. Remember, I'm a photographer," Bizzy added.

"Currently we're having a special on dog photography. Maybe you'd like to have Wolf photographed." Jacko said in one quick breath. Bizzy turned to him.

"I still want Wolf to do a portrait for me," Bizzy said.

"I told you, he'd eat your camera - after he ate you."

"That sweet Rottie would never eat anybody."

Wolf let out a low growl.

"We're sorry to bother you. Can I just come and get the ball?" Bizzy asked.

Schaeffer looked them both up and down, and Luigi sat down.

"What kind of dog is that?" He pointed to Luigi.

"He's a Doodle, a Labradoodle."

"Oh, one of those designer mutts. I have a purebred." He laughed and shouted back at the house. "Right, Wolfie?"

Wolf started his growling/barking again.

He pointed at Bizzy. "You can go in, but him and the dog need to stay out here."

"That's fine with me, us," Jacko said.

Bizzy gave the leash to Jacko and walked into the yard. It was dusk, and the sky was wearing its last pinkish-purple hues. The edges of night were encroaching on the evening. She turned back to Jacko, who shrugged. She pulled her phone from her pocket. "Okay, I'm just going to turn this light on," Bizzy announced to Schaeffer, who was still glaring at her.

"Do what you need to. Just get the ball and get out."

Wolf's growl made Bizzy clench her teeth. She put the phone up, and the light almost blinded her. She quickly turned the phone over, but it took a few seconds for her eyes to readjust. She moved the phone slowly from one side to the other as she walked. With the sunlight gone and the light of the phone casting shadows, all the shapes of the old boats, lobster traps, buoys, and other paraphernalia made the whole yard look like a twisted forest.

Then she saw a bunch of tall sticks. She moved toward them.

"Better not of break any of my pepper plants," Schaeffer grumbled at her. Wolf growled in agreement.

She moved her phone flashlight around and checked out the rest of the yard, which was also filled with seaside junk. Old wooden planks, beach chairs, even a collapsed rubber unicorn floaty. She held on it for a second. She saw the fence that separated Schaeffer's property from hers and Edy's. She noticed that nearly all the fence slats were weatherworn and dilapidated. But one section looked new compared to the rest of the fence. She walked over to it. More scrap metal and junk.

Then she glimpsed a slice of the orange ball a few feet

away. "I think I found it!" she announced as she walked over to the middle of the yard.

"You better watch where you step," Schaeffer said. Bizzy immediately put the light on the path directly in front of her. She gingerly stepped over some sharp-looking metal spikes that could easily puncture someone. She picked up the ball in the middle of the spikes and made the trek back to the fence.

"Mr. Schaeffer, did you replace a bit of the fence between our houses?"

"You just noticing now?"

"Yeah."

"Must have replaced it couple of years ago."

"I guess I wasn't paying attention."

Wolf lay beside Schaeffer as Bizzy walked back toward the gate. She got to the gate and picked up the latch, then glanced at her hands and noticed red smears. *Rust.*

"Thanks again, Mr. Schaeffer."

Schaeffer gave no reply, but Wolf barked an angry "get out of my yard and don't come back." Bizzy eyed Jacko and Luigi by the seawall. When Luigi saw her, he pulled toward her, but Jacko held tight to the leash. Luigi saw the ball and began to jump up and down, as if nothing nefarious had just transpired.

CHAPTER TWENTY

"What do you want?" The annoyed voice came over the phone, and she pressed speaker phone.

"Wow, Doug, good morning to you too. You sound tired." After a short pause, Bizzy went on. "Well, I have two questions. One is very practical. You said that you were finished with the crime scene, but Howie says *you* have to call him and say you're finished."

"We're finished."

"Great. Howie says nobody has called. Will you, or someone, call him?" She heard a grunt of agreement from the other end of the phone.

"Okay, thanks," Bizzy said. "Second question: Did you get in touch with Angela?"

It was very quiet. Bizzy looked down at her phone. "You still there?"

"Bizzy, can you just let me, and the police, do this?"

"Okay." She sucked on her bottom lip a little. "Can you tell me what the autopsy said?"

"That's three questions, not two. And how do you know the report's even back yet?"

Bizzy pulled the phone away from her ear and made a face at the phone. "I just figured." Bizzy smiled to herself. She *did* know people who knew people.

"Yes, it came back."

"What did Shirley find?"

"Bizzy, I'm in the middle of a murder investigation."

"Just tell me one thing: Was there dirt and mulch in his clothes or bones or whatever?"

After a moment Doug said, "As a matter of fact, yes."

"So what does that make you think?"

"Bizzy," Doug's voice was very condescending, "I think he was buried in dirt."

"Originally."

"Right."

"And you think the body was moved?"

"Yes."

"How was he killed?"

"Blunt-force trauma to the head."

"So he was hit with something in the head, and then buried. He *was* dead, right?"

"Yes, Bizzy."

"Why? Why did someone hit him on the head?"

"I don't know yet, Bizzy. I have this crazy lady calling with ideas about the case, so I can't get to it."

"Who would that be?"

He chuckled and then sighed. "Maybe you should join the force?"

"Too late. I think I'm too old. Plus, I'm not real big on blood or death, remember? I stopped taking photos of it because it was too much."

"You're still good at the photos."

"Listen, you need motive right now, right?" She could

feel him rolling his eyes. "That's why you have to contact Angela. Tony was involved in something."

"Bizzy! As for Angela, we can't find her."

"What?"

"Yeah, she's gone. Left. Unreachable."

"How's that possible?"

"She cleared out her bank account and disappeared. Maybe she took a vacation and didn't tell anyone where she was going."

"You think she had something to do with Tony's murder? But she was the one helping with the warden's investigation."

"I asked around, Bizzy, and I can't confirm that. You and Donny Smith are the only ones who think that."

"Angela seemed to..." She stopped talking. It was dawning on Bizzy that Angela might have scammed her and that she might have been involved in Tony's murder.

"Bizzy, I've got to get back to work. And I have to come up with some solid ideas for this case."

"Why would Angela meet with me?"

"Maybe because she wanted to see if you had any information. Anything concrete."

"But how then-"

"Bizzy, the dirt thing is good. Really good. But you might have scared off a witness. Or an accomplice."

"Oh, no."

She heard a loud sigh over the phone. "Bizzy, you just have to realize this is *not* your case. Okay?" His voice was much softer now.

"Did you-"

"I want you to stop asking questions."

"Okay," Bizzy relented.

She squinted and knew her face had a weird pinched-up look.

"Okay," she said again. The phone call ended.

Bizzy's fingers were crossed. She looked down at them. "Doug, just a few more questions."

∾

LATER THAT AFTERNOON, Bizzy came around the corner and saw Edy sitting in a long flowy dress around the other side of her property, facing the beach. She gingerly turned the pages of the book in her hand as she read. "I found my journal."

"That's awesome."

"I found it tucked away in Jay's old room."

Bizzy retrieved an old beach chair from the side of the house, expanded it, and sat across from Edy. "Did you write anything about what Tony was up to?"

"I wrote about our relationship." She went forward a little. "This little bit got to me: 'I think he must have lost interest in me. He seems to be so preoccupied with work. It feels familiar.'"

"Did you write anything about Angela?"

She went back and forth among the pages. "She doesn't come in until the end: 'Tony and I fought over Angela. I told him if he wanted to be with other people, he could go back to just being a tenant.' Of course, that was a lie."

"When did Angela start calling?"

Edy glanced up to her. "I don't understand?"

"I mean, when did she start calling in regards to when Tony went missing?"

Edy smiled. "I guess she called a lot just before he left." She sighed. "Of course, he didn't leave."

"Was it weeks," probed Bizzy, "or days before he left?"

"It started happening," she opened the book again, "around mid-September. He disappeared in October."

"Did you ever suspect Tony of cheating?"

"Not really. Or at least I didn't want to. But honestly those phone calls from Angela calls sowed some seeds of doubt in my mind. When I confronted him about the calls, he said they were strictly about work, and wouldn't say any more."

"So Angela started calling a couple of weeks before he left-"

"I think we can say 'died'. That's what happened."

"Yeah..." Bizzy looked down.

"You said that Tony was doing something for the warden."

"It seems to me that maybe Tony was trying to find evidence of guards bringing in contraband. Or not."

"Which is it?"

"Angela has disappeared. She withdrew a bunch of money. Emptied her bank account, in fact, and left."

"But you told me she was living in her parents' house or something."

"She *was*. I just drove over there now. A nephew said she left yesterday. He had been staying there with her and taking care of the house."

"I don't understand."

"Is there anything in your diaries or anything you remember that would lead you to believe that Tony was involved in something that might have been over his head, and he was killed for it?"

Edy opened the book again. "I will keep looking."

"Angela made it crystal clear that she was *not* having an

affair with Tony. But what if she was having an affair with someone else?"

Edy stared at her.

"Maybe," Bizzy continued, "maybe those phone calls were about setting him up."

"I will keep looking."

"Did Schaeffer and Tony hang out?"

"Not really. As I recall, they were constantly pissed at each other. Schaeffer said that Tony's fixing of the original fence was destroying his flowers on the other side. You remember how weird Schaeffer was when we were putting the new deck in."

"He had flowers there?" Bizzy asked.

"Maybe. I've haven't been over there in a long time."

"I have. The yard is big, but it's filled with junk."

"At one point, a long, long time ago he definitely kept a nicer yard. Grew veggies." Edy sighed. "I use to get big bags of veggies on my doorstep."

Bizzy smiled, "Did he have a crush on you?"

Edy looked out for a minute, then shook her head. "He might have, but I don't think so. He was just *nice* a long time ago."

"Nice to Tony?" Bizzy asked.

"I'm not sure that I would go *that* far." Edy was now fanning through the book, and a photo dropped to the ground. Bizzy knew immediately it was a photo of Edy and Tony. Edy scooped it up and looked at the photo. "A long time ago."

"Can I see?" Bizzy put her hand out.

Edy stuck the photo to her heart. "Ah, sure." She handed Bizzy the photo.

Tony looked like a young Al Pacino, and his arms enveloped a younger Edy. Her head was back against his chest in mid-laugh as he kissed her cheek. "Stunning. Both of you - so gorgeous."

Edy looked like she was recreating the moment in front of her eyes. "Yes. He had the sweetest heart." She glanced back at the photo. "I always thought he left me. It hurt so bad, because I didn't know why."

"He didn't," Bizzy whispered. "And from what others have told me, he never would have."

She opened the book and stuck the photo back in. She read the page as she was inserting the photo and continued reading the diary.

"So, about four days before he left, I wrote: 'Tony told me third shifts would all be over. He would be back to regular shifts. I asked him if that would be the end of it?' I kept thinking of the woman calling him."

"Okay, what was his answer, Edy?"

"He said he hoped that night was his last third shift." Edy continued to read: "'I asked him if he might get a raise or promotion or something.' The next day "she" calls. I asked him who "she" was. He tells me, the warden's secretary.'"

Edy laughed. "I wrote in the margin: 'Fred Long keeps coming over and saying hi.'"

"So *Fred* was into you?" Bizzy asked.

She shook her head. "I don't think so. He told me later that he thought Tony was no good. That he was a two-timer."

"He went out of his way to tell you this?"

"Keep in mind, he and his wife had divorced a few months before, and I thought he was just being friendly 'cause he was lonely."

"Hmm. I never thought of him as lonely."

"I told him Tony was fine."

She breathed in. "I've gone over everything in my mind a million times. Now I'm not sure. Tony was working third shift, and he had slept in late that day. We fought, because, while he was asleep, Angela called."

"What did she say?"

"To tell Tony the meeting was still on."

"Did he talk about any meeting?"

"No, but he did take a rain slicker that night. It wasn't raining, and there wasn't any rain in the forecast." Edy's eyes didn't focus on Bizzy at all. "He was really short with me. I asked him why he was taking the coat. And he said not to worry." She smiled. "I remember him picking up Jay and telling him that he was going to make him proud. That's all I remember."

Bizzy wiped her eyes. "I think he was doing something important. I think he wanted to catch some criminal activity, and he might have died doing that."

"I hate to think that sweet, sweet man died in vain."

"I think Angela is the key here."

"How so?"

"Everyone has mentioned her. She was the warden's secretary, and was privy to the warden's plans. Evidently plans that Tony was a part of. I'm betting she knows the missing pieces to this puzzle."

Edy could hear the wheels turning in Bizzy's head. "And?"

"And just maybe, somehow she is the reason why Tony got killed that night."

CHAPTER TWENTY-ONE

Jacko stood at the stove with Luigi by his side. Bizzy didn't mean to storm in, but when the screen door slammed behind her, Jacko jumped. "What's going on?"

"What are you cooking? It smells amazing."

"Just a little something you said you like."

"Lobster? Chicken Saltimbocca? Fajitas?"

His face fell. "Eggplant parmigiana." He said the parmigiana with an Italian accent.

"I love eggplant parmigiana!"

He turned around to the stove. "I saw you talking to Edy."

"You did?"

"Luigi wanted to go with you, but I could tell you two didn't need any interruptions."

"Thanks for that. I know she's told the police everything, but I just kept probing. I think Angela is the key."

The eggplant sizzled in the cast iron pan. Bizzy loved it fried, but was always looking to lose some calories. As the scent wafted through the air and she saw Jacko at the stove, she felt a wave of peace rush through her body.

It is a good thing that Jacko is here.

And then Dan came back to her mind, and her heart hurt.

"I was wondering if you'd go back over with me to Fred Long's house?"

"Why?"

"I think he knows more than he's telling."

"Why do you think he will tell us anything?"

"Because Fred is a big flirt and a busybody. I have never known him *not* to know everyone's business. And then he goes around gossiping. But he's been real quiet on this."

"Maybe it was such a long time ago that he doesn't remember," Jacko said. He flipped the breaded goodness over one last time. Bizzy saw the sauce bubbling and the grated cheese all ready to go.

"Or maybe he does remember and needs some convincing."

"Okay." He put a little sauce in the glass baking dish, then carefully put the fried eggplant in. Jacko ladled some more sauce over it, then healthy doses of two different types of cheese. He popped it in the oven.

Bizzy watched Jacko as if he were producing a TV show called *Cooking for Bizzy.* "You can really cook," she said with amazement.

"Can't really take the credit for that. Nonna made sure everyone could cook. She was afraid the boys would marry girls who couldn't cook. Then where would I be?"

Bizzy laughed. "What you meant to say is, Nonna was afraid you'd marry a non-Italian, non-cooking girl."

He smirked. "Gotta give her credit for that. She wanted

her grandson to be prepared for the worst. Back to Fred. What do you think?" Jacko asked.

"I think he knows something. He has to. His stories have all sorts of details about people, whether it's from last week or thirty years ago."

"The only one who's not nice is Schaeffer."

"Yeah, Edy says at one time Schaeffer was nice. Sweet, even."

Jacko pointed in the direction of Schaeffer's house. "*That* guy? With growling, man-and-woman-eating Wolf?"

"Brought her veggies from his garden."

Jacko put a timer on. "I'm going to check the eggplant in 20 minutes to see where we are at."

"Come with me to Fred Long's."

Jacko looked at her. "Same M.O. as last time?"

"I actually think we can skip the throwing the ball in his yard. We can knock."

"Okay. But after we finish dinner."

Bizzy nodded. "Deal. By the way, Doug said the police are done with the crime scene, so they will call Howie and tell him that the crew can come back to the project."

"Awesome."

Bizzy got the leash and a ball, and said, "I am going to take this puppy out to the beach for a quick run so he doesn't spend all dinnertime begging."

"Perfect," Jacko replied. "Dinner will be on the table when you get back."

Bizzy took Luigi out, and went over the ramp to the beach. Bizzy started running, and Luigi kept pace with her. Then he saw an Australian shepherd puppy friend of his on the beach, and begged Bizzy to let him play chase with his friend. But Bizzy said: "Sorry, Luigi. Another time. We have to head back, because dinner is on the table. And I will feed you your dinner too."

"Smells good," Bizzy said to Jacko as she walked in the door. She picked up a piece of garlic bread and took a big bite. "That is a *lot* of garlic."

"That's bad?"

"Nope. Absolutely delicious."

He put plates of pasta on the table. "Mangia."

"Don't mind if I do." She sat down. "So what were we talking about?"

"Fred Long. What are we going to talk to him about?"

"I've talked to him, but I want to ask a few questions about Angela." Bizzy took a bite of the eggplant parmesan. "Mmmm. This is really good," she said, with her mouth full. "You can cook for me anytime."

She noticed Jacko looking at her. He smiled. Then he picked up his fork and dug into his mound of pasta.

While they were eating, Jacko said, "Why don't we go over what we know so far?"

"Good idea. Donny says Tony was one of the good guys, but there was something going on in the jail. Angela admits that there was something going on, and Tony was involved, getting info for the Warden. But now she has disappeared, and nobody knows where. Schaeffer is definitely still a front-running suspect. He used to have a big vegetable garden and still has some remnants amidst his yard full of junk."

"Schaeffer is meaner than a junkyard dog. And he *has* one."

"I think Wolf *could* be a sweet dog. He just keeps bad company is all."

"So what about Fred?"

"I just *know* Fred knows something. He knows all sorts of things about everyone but isn't saying anything. Is he trying to protect someone? Would he try to protect Schaeffer? I don't think they're friends, but..."

~

AFTER DINNER, Bizzy and Jacko took the dog and headed to Fred's house. "So we're just going to ask him a few questions and leave, right?" Jacko asked as they approached.

"Yup. That's it."

"And why am I here?" There was a slight twinge of whine in Jacko's voice.

"Crime-fighting partner, remember?"

"Do not refer to me as Robin."

"I wasn't going to." She looked down at Luigi. "He's Scooby, and you're Shaggy."

"I think I'd rather be Robin."

Bizzy laughed, but then put her hand over her mouth. "Shhh..."

"Do we *have* to be quiet?" asked Jacko.

Bizzy shook her head.

Fred Long's house was situated on the street, was well kept, and he had flower boxes outside the little windows. Bizzy remembered seeing him build them. They fit his tiny house. Fred didn't own his home, but he had lived there for a long time, renting. She could remember Dan saying that some people just liked renting. He didn't understand it, and Bizzy certainly didn't. "Big waste of money," she had said.

Bizzy would have regarded Fred's house as a shack, if not for the fact that Fred kept it so neat. Before she could even knock, Fred opened the door.

"Bizzy, how are you?"

"Good, Fred. Good."

"Jacko and I were just walking Luigi here. A thought came to me about Tony."

"Yeah, Tony. Nice guy."

"Yeah, everyone keeps saying that."

"Can I invite you in?"

"Maybe go around back? Our shoes are all sandy."

"Sure, sure, I never have people sit at my back table. And I bought a brand new one, too."

Fred had a small wooden fence, and the gate latch was broken. Bizzy pulled the gate open to let herself, Jacko, and Luigi in. The back yard was tiny but well organized.

"You do quite a lot with such a little space," Jacko said. They both looked around and saw a ton of veggies ready to be harvested.

"My favorite time of the year - when you see all the fruits of your labor."

Bizzy glanced around the yard, decorated in a nautical motif. Oars were scattered in different places and hung on the walls of his shed.

"You like oars," noticed Jacko.

"Love them. From way back when," Fred's hand twirled in a way that told them they were going back in history, "my grandfather use to row to the jail, where he worked in maintenance. And my father worked there, too. They always used to row over, but then the county put the road in. So rowing wasn't really necessary after that."

Bizzy turned to Jacko. "At one time, there was a space between the island and the mainland," she explained with a chuckle. "As if we are 'the mainland.'"

"We were!" said Fred, his blue eyes blazing.

"I guess." She looked around. "Are these oars the ones your father and grandfather used?"

"Yeah. Some of them are. And now some I just collect."

Most of the oars were in sets of two, except one that stood all by itself. "Only one?" Bizzy asked.

"Lost the other," said Fred. "Lost it rowing with a nephew. He dropped it, and it sank into the ocean."

"Surprised you didn't go dive for it."

Fred narrowed his eyes at her. "Didn't want the kid to feel bad. That was a long time ago."

They settled themselves onto the furniture. Bizzy bounced on the cushion. "Wow, these are brand new!"

"Yeah," Fred smiled, "like I told you."

Fred had put three glasses and a pitcher of water on the table. Bizzy pulled one of the glasses toward her and then picked up the pitcher and poured.

"Can I ask you a few more questions about Tony?"

"Yeah, I guess. Seems to be a theme around here. With the police and all. Funny after all these years, it's hard to remember what he looked like."

"You said he was a nice guy. Was he involved – dating - the warden's secretary, Angela?"

"Don't know. Maybe. Though I think he had his eye on Edy."

"Did Tony know of some bad stuff going on at the jail?"

Fred laughed. "We all knew there was some bad stuff going on at the jail. It was a jail, after all."

Bizzy smiled, "Was there stuff going on with the guards? You know, like, selling stuff?"

"I don't know. As I told the police, there were guys trying to make a few bucks on the side. You know, for an alimony payment or..."

"Were you paying alimony, Fred?"

"I was, but I was just putting that in as an example." He flashed that smile again. Fred always knew how to charm people.

"Was Schaeffer involved?"

He shrugged. "Who knows with Bertie? He was always odd. His Jeannie died, and he became a recluse."

"He didn't get involved with other people?"

"Nah. He didn't like anyone. He didn't get involved."

"So chances are, he didn't do anything illegal?"

"Chances are."

"Did you think Tony was?"

Fred didn't say anything for a long while. He coughed, then sipped some water. "Don't know. Didn't seem the type. Cause he was all straight-laced and all."

"Who could have been involved in whatever was going on?"

"There were a couple of guys I think would have made good candidates. We use to joke that the only difference between the prisoners and those guards was which side of the bars they were on."

Bizzy got up and walked around. "Gosh, some of these oars are old. Antique-like, huh?" She pulled out her phone and put it up to snap a shot of some oars decoratively hanging on Fred's house. Fred pushed her hand down.

"Ah, don't take pictures. You'd probably put them on social media or something, and I don't want that."

"I'm sorry, Fred, I should have asked." She returned the phone to her pocket.

"Ah, no problem. I've heard stories of all that internet stuff."

Bizzy walked toward the gate. "Well, thanks for the chat." Jacko followed her with the dog.

They walked back to the seawall and climbed up a staircase over the wall, then descended onto the beach. Silence filled the space between them.

"You know what I think?" Bizzy asked.

"No, but I'm sure I'm going to hear it."

CHAPTER TWENTY-TWO

The next afternoon, Bizzy walked into the police station. Doug Williams was chatting with a group of officers, and they all shared a collective laugh. Then one of them pointed to Bizzy. Doug turned around and rolled his eyes, then started to walk toward her.

"Did you just roll your eyes at me?" Bizzy asked.

"Don't take offense, you, the latest amateur detective in our ranks." He laughed. "We really don't need anyone else."

"I don't know," Bizzy fired back, "you're always claiming to be understaffed."

"How can I help you, Bizzy Devlin?" Doug's usual scowl had returned.

"You said a blunt-force trauma, right?"

Doug nodded.

"What kind of object would it have been?"

"Blunt force means something hard hit the person to cause trauma to some part of the body. We don't know the environment, what would have been available to the murderer."

The rest of the officers were glaring at Doug and Bizzy.

Doug took Bizzy by the elbow. "Let's go to my office, and I'll explain all about blunt-force trauma."

Bizzy wrangled out of the elbow hold and followed him down the hall to his office. She sat down in the chair across from his desk. Doug sat down, too. He pulled a folder from his rack, opened it, and glanced at some of the information.

"So you want to know about blunt-force trauma?"

"Yes, I do. I am trying to wrap my head around what kind of weapon could have been used."

"It could have been a hundred different things: a baseball bat, a rock, a shovel. Shirley seems to think it was most likely something flat."

"Can I read the file?"

"Absolutely not." He put the folder back in the rack.

"What does it say?" She leaned forward, putting her hands on the edge of the desk.

"It says people who are not professional law enforcement should not get involved."

Bizzy laughed. "I know you made that up." She knew this was Doug's way of being cheeky.

"Bizzy, leave this alone. It's bad enough I get to be haunted by all this." He leaned forward on his desk. "I seem to recall that someone stopped taking photos of crime scenes, because she couldn't handle it anymore."

"That last one... Dan thought - I thought - it might have been time to give it up. I had nightmares." Bizzy noticed her hands shook.

"Listen, Biz, I'm saying this for your own good." His voice was soft. Almost the Doug she remembered.

"Doug, I realize I was thinking about the different levels of sand and what it meant about the placement of the body, and I was wrong about that. You were right."

Doug smiled. "And?"

"But between the day before the deck was finished and the next day, the photos show a definite difference in the color of the ground. One day there was only sand, and the very next day there was dark earth and mulch in the same spot that the body was later found."

"I know you want to exonerate your friend, but anyone could manipulate that."

"Doug, I could also have Photoshopped a handsome face onto your picture. But I wouldn't."

He pointed to the door. "Out, Devlin."

BIZZY PRACTICALLY RAN to her car, doing a half jog, half walk and tapping the fob to open the door way before she needed to. She could hear the locks click. She got in and fumbled with her phone. The car finally recognized her phone.

"Name the person you'd like to call," the robotic voice commanded.

"Jacko."

The ringing came through the speaker. One ring, two rings. "Come on, Jacko."

"Hey, Biz."

"Jacko, are you at the house?"

"Yeah."

"Good. Don't move."

"I wasn't planning to. Don't forget we have a shoot today out on the beach."

"We do?"

"Bizzy, we've talked about this."

"Okay, okay. What time?"

"In five minutes. It's almost golden hour."

"I'll be home in five minutes." Jacko started to moan. "Okay, hanging up."

~

SHE PARKED in the lot near her home and locked the car. Now she did a full-on gallop up the boardwalk to the house. When she arrived, Jacko was outside.

"I'm here." She smiled.

"Great. I am going to go down to the beach. Kevin and Apollo are already there waiting. You just need to get your camera and see if the camera settings are right. We'll need to leave Luigi with Edy."

When Bizzy walked in the house, Luigi started jumping on her. "Hey, baby, you have to stay here, because Mommy has to go photograph another dog. Not as cute as you. But a cute dog that thinks he might be a horse."

Bizzy picked up her camera from the counter and checked the settings. She made sure she had her long lens on her camera to shoot Apollo and Kevin from a distance, since she had already been showered in drool at the studio session a few days before. Even so, she wore a raincoat, just in case.

She walked out the door, and Luigi slipped out to follow her. Bizzy knocked on Edy's door and called out, "Edy, can I ask you to take Lou for a little while? We have a shoot on the beach. This shouldn't take too long. The light is starting to fade, anyway."

"No problem, Bizzy. Aunt Edy will take good care of my sweet puppy-nephew, Lulu."

Bizzy headed down to the beach as she waved in gratitude. "Be back soon, Edy.

~

BIZZY AND JACKO walked back from the photoshoot laughing. "Even with your raincoat, Apollo still got you with his flying drool!" Jacko said.

"My hair! Ugh! He got my hair! I am going to need a towel to wipe off the drool."

"At least you saved the camera."

Bizzy sniffed the air. "What's that smell? Jacko, did you leave something on the stove?"

"No. I always turn off the burners. Except when I don't."

She sniffed the air again. "Fire. Is someone having a bonfire on the beach?" Bizzy glanced up and down the beach. She didn't see any fires anywhere. She looked around at the houses. She could see smoke and an orange glow coming from the direction of Fred Long's house.

Schaeffer came to his fence with Wolf beside him.

"It looks like Fred Long's house," she said to Jacko and Schaeffer, pointing to Fred's house.

Jacko said, "We need to call the fire department."

"Don't bother," grumbled Schaeffer, "it looks like he is just burning trash."

"If he's burning trash," Bizzy called back, "the whole neighborhood could go up in flames!"

She turned to Jacko. "Jacko, call the fire department. I am going to tell Fred to put it out."

"My phone is in the house," Jacko said. "I will go make the call."

Bizzy ran toward the fire.

"Fred! Fred!" Bizzy shouted. She frantically rushed through the broken gate and into the back yard. Fred was in front of a blazing fire, his oars stacked up.

"What are you doing?" Bizzy cried. "You know you can't have a fire here!"

He threw in another oar, and it crackled as sparks flew into the sky.

"You're putting everybody in danger," Bizzy persisted.

She noticed all the oars had vanished from the fence and their decorative arrangements in a pile.

The gears started turning in Bizzy's head, and some pieces of the puzzle finally came together for her.

Bizzy turned the camera to video and pressed a button to record.

"Don't come near me," Fred warned her. "And don't take any pictures."

"Why are you burning all your beloved oars?"

He looked back at her. His eyes had a strange mix of calm and demented determination. He went to get another oar.

"Get out of here, Bizzy. These are my oars. I can do whatever I want with them." She looked at the oars and realized that the most prized ones hanging on the walls of his house were still intact.

The fire crackled as Fred picked up another oar and broke it in half. He was about to throw it into the fire.

"Don't!" Bizzy cried. "She pulled her phone out of her pocket "You're destroying..."

Fred no longer had his usual sweet look. His eyes bulged, and some of the soot from the fire streaked his face.

"You're destroying evidence."

He picked up another oar, but now he was making his way toward Bizzy with it. She backed up. "I told you to get out of here!"

"Listen, you can't do this." Bizzy hit Jacko's number on the phone.

"What's up, Bizzy?" Jacko's voice came through faintly.

"Who's that?" asked Fred as he looked around trying to find the source of the voice.

"It's Jacko. He's calling the police right now."

"There will be no way they can prove anything."

"The oar. You killed him with the oar."

Fred looked down at the one in his hand. "This was my father's. He used it to row to the island." He started to walk toward Bizzy.

Bizzy stepped back. "What happened?" she asked.

Fred smiled at her and took another step toward her. "You want to know what happened?" Fred asked.

"It was an accident, wasn't it?"

"What makes you think it was me?"

"Did Angela help you?"

Fred laughed. In the distance Bizzy heard the faint sound of a siren.

"Ever kill anyone?" Fred asked.

Bizzy shook her head. "Why did you kill Tony?"

"You think I killed him? You have that thing taping me?" He stepped closer to her.

He swung the oar, whacked her hand, and the phone flew to the ground. Bizzy screamed. She looked around the yard and realized she was trapped, cut off from the gate. And if she went the other way, she was deeper in the yard with the plants and vegetables.

Fred found the phone and stepped on it.

"I was taping you," she said. "I called Jacko..."

He was only a few steps from her. She could see that now his mouth was foaming with rage.

"Tony was just plain nosy. Kind of like you."

"You think I'm nosy?"

"I think that you're a *Bizzy* body."

Bizzy realized if she let him swing, he might be so off balance she could grab hold of the oar, and that might be her only chance. Fred was coming closer.

Okay, come a little closer. "So he was nosy, huh?"

"Working for the warden. So, yeah. He was nosy."

The picture was getting clearer in Bizzy's mind. "He found out it was you who was selling contraband to the prisoners."

Fred smiled at her, and he took another step toward her. "Oh, I was selling a bunch of stuff. You name it. I was making good money for the first time ever." He motioned with the oar all around the yard. "I wanted to make this little bit of paradise mine."

"Did Angela know?"

Fred stepped closer. He cackled as he looked down at the oar. "Angela liked men. So she and I used to snuggle sometimes. And she got a little chatty when we were snuggling. Without intending to, she let me know that the warden had Tony helping him."

"So what happened?"

"We still had boats, you know. And I would row out to the outskirts of the island and put stuff in the boathouse. Since I am a friendly sort of guy, Tony let me into his confidence. He told me that he was working for the warden. So I told Tony I was pretty sure Schaeffer was the guy doing the contraband. And I offered to take Tony to where I thought the stash was. He said that maybe we could go to the warden together. I said we had to go and see it for ourselves first."

"And he believed you."

"Oh yeah, he swallowed it, hook, line, and sinker. We rowed out to the old boathouse together, and he saw the stash. I told him, 'Maybe we can get a piece of the action.'"

"But Tony didn't want any part of it, did he?"

"Nope. Just wanted to tell the warden all about it and be done with it. Too bad for him. He should have played along. So, as we were going back to the rowboat, I hit him with the oar. My grandpa's oar, one of the ones that's burning up right now."

Bizzy moved back another step, and then she felt her foot hit something. She lost her balance and started to fall backwards. As she reached out, her hand grabbed at a stick, and it splintered in her hand. She could feel the sharp wood tear the skin on her arm as she fell. A stinging pain ran up her arm.

"What are you doing?" screamed Fred. "Those are my tomatoes!"

She pulled the stick out of the ground, and she heard the splat as the tomatoes hit the dirt. "Geez, so you hit him in the back of the head, huh? As he was walking on the rocks?"

"I'm not actually sure if the oar killed him or not. But falling down head first onto the rocks definitely finished him off."

Bizzy could hear the sound of sirens approaching. But she was more focused on Fred as he stepped toward her.

Fred smiled a devilish grin. "I rowed back to my car with his body, and I drove right home. Got him out in the dead of night. And no one ever suspected. I couldn't believe how easy it was. It was a dream."

Bizzy could feel the blood dripping off of her hands, but she dared not look. "A dream. Sure. How'd you look Edy in the eye?"

He smiled. "Easy. She's a beautiful woman."

"You killed the love of her life."

"Like I said, he should have played along."

"So you moved the body from here to our deck when we replaced it."

He tapped the side of his head with his forefinger. "Smart, eh?"

She shook her head. "Not how I'd describe it."

"Sure it was. Edy was out of town. I had to buy those Red Sox tickets to get you all out of the house. And they were expensive. But I knew Dan and Jay couldn't resist, and you would go along. Everything fell right into place."

"Then you planted hostas there. With the dirt and mulch that Tony had been buried in. Just in case, huh?"

She tightened her hand around the stick. Fred moved a small step. "So you are going to kill me, too?"

Fred smiled broadly. "Well, neighbor, now I have to."

"How do you think you're going to get away with it?"

"Well, I was burning my old oars, and you snuck up on me. In the darkness I was startled and hit the intruder before I realized it was Bizzy Devlin."

"They'll never believe you."

"Sure they will. I'm Fred Long. Everybody knows I'm a nice guy."

"Oh my," Bizzy said.

"All Tony had to do was go along. And not be some boy scout."

Fred jumped forward.

Now, if he swings...

He swung. Bizzy caught the oar with one hand and jabbed the stick at him, puncturing his arm.

Fred let out a blood-curdling scream.

"Help! Help!" Bizzy called out at the top of her lungs. She pushed Fred back, and he fell into his garden, smashing his beloved tomato plants. In the light of the fire she could see him writhing in the patch, trying to get his balance to get up. His arm was limp now and was no help to his cause.

She heard a rustling sound. Bizzy just screamed at the top of her lungs. "Over here!" Just then Wolf charged into the yard and leapt onto Fred. He growled ferociously and barked at him, snapping his jowls when Fred tried to move.

"It's your word against mine," laughed Fred. "You'll have to prove it."

"No she won't," said a gruff voice. Bertie Schaeffer walked over and grabbed the leash of his dog. "I heard everything."

"I'm sorry, Schaeffer. I thought it was you," Bizzy said.

They heard the sound of more voices.

"Over here, in Fred Long's yard!" Schaeffer called out.

Doug came in first, his gun drawn, followed by a bunch of uniformed officers. He saw Bizzy with the stick in her hand, blood dripping. "Call an ambulance."

Fred tried to get up and run, but Wolf grabbed him by the arm and hung on tightly. "Get this mutt off me! He's going to rip my arm off."

"Maybe he should," Schaeffer said. "Don't tempt me."

"You can call the dog off, Mr. Schaeffer," Doug said. Schaeffer took Wolf by the collar and pulled him back. "Good Wolf."

Doug removed the oar from Fred's hand and saw his wound. "Make that two ambulances."

Doug said looking at the flow of blood down Bizzy's arm. "Doesn't look that bad."

She glanced down and realized what he was seeing. "It's my blood."

Doug took out a handkerchief and put it on her wound. He was holding her arm up. Jacko came running in with a towel.

"Sit down, Bizzy, sit down." He guided her to an Adirondack chair. Wolf came over and looked at her.

"Hi, Wolfie." The dog put his head down on her lap. "I always knew you were a sweetheart." She stroked his head with her good hand.

More cops came and an ambulance arrived on the scene soon after.

Two EMTs surrounded Bizzy. One of them said, "You are going to need something before the pain sets in. Let me give you a shot."

Two others took Fred away on a gurney. Doug and Schaeffer were talking. Bizzy was still petting Wolf with her good hand.

Suddenly, Bizzy heard Edy's voice. "Where is she?" Luigi barked.

Bizzy turned around. Edy shook her head and rushed for her. "What happened?"

Bizzy started telling Edy what had happened, with Jacko filling in details that Bizzy skipped over. The EMTs attending Bizzy brought in another gurney.

"Seriously, I don't think I need that."

"Well, Nancy Drew," Doug's authoritative voice powered over everyone, "you *will* be going to the Hospital. And you *will* be getting it looked at." She let Jacko and the EMTs help her to the stretcher. Before they raised her up, Wolf came over and licked her face.

"Wolf, when I come home, will you play with Luigi? He really needs a friend." He licked her again. Then she turned to Schaeffer. "Hey, Schaeffer, I need to thank you."

"Don't mention it. I mean that. I don't want anyone to think I'm getting soft in my old age." He gave her a wink and a little wave as the EMTs secured her and then raised the stretcher bed. She passed Jacko, holding onto Luigi's leash.

She could see that Luigi was yelping and whining for her, but she couldn't really hear.

The stretcher wobbled and crunched over the uneven ground, but Bizzy never knew. The pain medicine kicked in, and she was asleep before the stretcher reached the ambulance.

CHAPTER TWENTY-THREE

Around 8 o'clock the following morning, Bizzy slowly walked up the boardwalk to her house, still a little groggy. Jacko wrapped one arm around her waist and steadied her as she walked.

"Okay, nice and easy," Jacko said.

"Where's Luigi?"

"Edy has him."

"Oh, I'm going to have to get a new phone."

"Well, it won't be that bad."

"I don't know whose numbers I have or don't have. And I don't back up..."

Jacko laughed, "Usually the phone backs up your numbers for you. It's magic, Bizzy."

They came to her house, and she stepped onto the sand. "I guess Howie and the boys will be starting the renovations soon."

"Yeah. They'll be on the job first thing Monday," said Jacko.

Edy came to her door, and below her Luigi was shaking,

barking, and scratching the door to get out. "He missed his mommy," Edy said.

"Hi, baby boy. Mama's back," Bizzy said.

"As soon as you are settled, I'll bring him over."

They were in the house, and Jacko led her to the couch. "What do you need?"

"Nothing. I mean, they gave me painkillers. They gave me stiches."

"Twenty-seven stiches. You realize that, right? Twenty-seven!"

"Yeah. It kind of throbs."

"You gouged your arm all the way from your wrist to your elbow. You are lucky you didn't hit an artery."

Bizzy looked down at her arm. It was mostly covered by an ace bandage, but underneath were more bandages she could see at the wrist. "I think this is going to hurt for a while."

"Yeah, you're going to have to take it easy."

Edy opened the door. "Is she all set? This guy needs to see his mama."

"Bring him in," said Bizzy.

"Keep him on the leash," Jacko said.

They both came in, Luigi trying desperately to get to Bizzy, almost pulling Edy's arm off. She protected her arm with the pillows on the sofa.

"Okay, wild man, come on."

Edy let him go, and he jumped on the couch, licking and trying to get as close as possible. Both Edy and Jacko held Luigi when he looked like he was going to get too close to the wounded arm. Finally, he calmed down and snuggled as close to Bizzy as he could.

"I think Wolf is going to be your new friend," she whispered.

Both Edy and Jacko were in the kitchen. Edy brought over a cup of tea and placed it within easy reach.

"Well, once this renovation thing gets rolling, it will take on a life of its own."

Edy sat across from her and looked intently at her. "I appreciate what you did, girl, I do."

Bizzy nodded and pulled the cup of tea to her face. "I know. You would have done the same for me."

"How did you figure out it was Fred?"

She looked into her cup. "The dirt."

"Dirt?" Edy asked.

"Yeah, the dirt and the mulch." Bizzy put the cup down and then lay back. "Tony," she started, watching Edy's face for any sign of discomfort. Edy nodded for her to go on. "Tony was buried in dirt and mulch. I took the pictures, and it showed dirt and mulch was still there on his body. 25 years later. But between our houses we've only had sand."

Edy nodded. "Yes, that's right."

"Anyway, Fred saw that we were redoing the deck. And figured he'd get rid of the body that he originally buried in his own yard." Edy's eyes showed a flash of sadness as Bizzy said "the body." Bizzy stopped.

"Go on, Bizzy," said Edy. "I need to hear this."

"Anyway, he talked Schaeffer into getting a whole new load of dirt, and mulch for their plants. They shared the dirt and mulch. All of this at the same time we were doing the deck. He figured none of us would notice when he moved Tony's body and reburied it under the deck. And we didn't." Bizzy put her cup down.

"Schaeffer told me that the dirt was supposed to be something special," said Jacko. "But nothing really grew as well as before. So a couple of years later, he got brand new dirt."

Luigi snuggled with Edy, then up on the couch with Bizzy, and went down to be patted by Jacko. He was doing the rounds.

They all jumped when they heard a soft knock. Doug was at the door.

"May I come in?" asked Doug to Jacko.

"Bizzy?" Jacko asked, turning to Bizzy for approval.

"Sure. Come on in, Doug."

Doug walked over to stand in front of Bizzy and Edy. Luigi jumped up on him.

"Down, Lou, down." Bizzy commanded, but her voice was a little weak.

Doug scanned her arm from the elbow to the wrist. "Jeez Bizzy, you did a good job. I heard it was like a hundred stitches."

"Twenty-seven!" Bizzy, Jacko, and Edy all said in unison and then laughed.

Doug smiled. "Twenty-seven is still impressive."

He stood there shifting from foot to foot.

"Sit down, Doug," said Bizzy.

"No, I just came by to tell you that Fred Long did confess. He knew that Schaeffer had heard it, so he said, 'Well, I've gotten away with it long enough.'"

Edy put her head down. "Got away with it?"

"Well, he won't be getting away with it anymore." Doug's face fell, and he continued shifting his weight from foot to foot. "Bizzy, you did a good job with the photos and all."

"Well, I *am* a photographer." Bizzy smiled.

"Yeah, but Nosy Nancy-"

"Why does everybody call any female detective-"

"Amateur sleuth," Doug said firmly. "Yeah, there aren't

that many, and I think you're a little young for Miss Marple."

Bizzy laughed and nodded. "Ok, I'll take Nancy."

"I called her Velma," said Jacko.

Doug stared at him.

"Scooby Doo?" Jacko asked.

"Okay, who's Velma?"

"Shaggy's girlfriend. The smart girl, not the good-looking girl."

Bizzy glared at him. "A girl can be smart *and* good looking. But I guess I'll just stick with Nancy, then."

Doug raised his index finger and wagged it her. "No more Nancy."

Bizzy smiled. "I hope so, Doug."

"I'll be leaving now, so get some rest. I am going to need you to come to the station and make a statement," Doug said.

"Ok," said Bizzy, "tomorrow."

"When you can," said Doug gently. Jacko and Luigi followed him to the door. He exited, and Jacko shut the door firmly.

Edy noticed Jacko shutting the door and asked, "Who do you think is coming?"

"I don't know," said Jacko. "I just wanted Bizzy to feel safe." The dog jumped on the couch and resumed his snuggle position with Bizzy.

"I'm going to leave. Get some sleep," said Edy as she looked over at Jacko. "Let me know if you need any help with this one." She pointed to Bizzy. "I'm pretty sure she's going to be a bad patient."

"Well, I was just about to give her some pain meds," said Jacko.

"I don't want them," said Bizzy. "Just give me--"

Edy nodded toward Jacko, "See what I mean?"

BIZZY AND JACKO walked on the beach. "I'm not going to fall, Jacko, I swear."

Luigi barreled toward them with the ball in his mouth. Jacko moved in front of Bizzy to cut off Luigi and protect her. Bizzy smiled. It was a nice gesture.

"So they're going to start the renovation tomorrow," said Bizzy.

"That's great, right?"

"I was wondering if you wanted to be like my Owner Project Manager."

"What's that?" He asked as he threw the ball far down the beach.

"That's a title I just came up with." Bizzy laughed. "Maybe I didn't."

"Meaning?"

"Well, you help me, or - who am I kidding - you run the renovation, and in return..."

Jacko looked at her, so Bizzy continued. "In return I'll give you a discount on room and board. You'll be my tenant who does stuff."

"How much rent?"

"I don't know. What's fair?" Bizzy said.

"Room *and* board?" asked Jacko.

"Yeah, I don't want to have two separate food preparations going on. None of that. Basically, I want you to cook." Bizzy glanced out at the ocean. "Is that something you want?"

Jacko smiled. "I'll take the job."

"Of course, I'll pay you separately for photography business stuff."

"Sounds great."

"Same rate."

Jacko nodded. "It all sounds good, Bizzy."

Luigi came barreling back at them again, his ears flapping in the wind.

They both laughed.

"He's so cute, Jacko. He was a good idea."

"See, I have them," Jacko said.

"Have what?"

"Good ideas."

"Yes you do, Shaggy."

"Aw, come on, I don't want to be Shaggy."

Luigi stopped in front of them and dropped the ball. He sat there and waited.

"Better throw the ball," Bizzy said.

Jacko threw the ball, and a gust of wind lifted the ball to the side, causing it to fall into the ocean. All three of them stared at the ball bobbing near the shore.

Jacko looked down at Luigi. "Go on Luigi. Go get the ball." Luigi went to the edge of the ocean, but a small wave lapped at his feet and he backed away, barking at it.

"He doesn't go into the water," Bizzy said.

"What about the ball?"

Now Luigi was barking louder at the ball bobbing up and down.

"Somebody has to go get it." Bizzy smiled and lifted her bandaged arm. "Unfortunately, it can't be me."

"The dog is supposed to-" They both looked at Luigi going forward, then backward when the wave came in, barking louder and louder.

"Oh, for Pete's sake!" Jacko took off his shoes and socks

and stood at the edge of the water. "Aw, man," he groaned as he started to walk into the ocean. "This is freezing!"

Bizzy laughed. Luigi watched as Jacko went in, but only followed him as far as the water's edge. Luigi watched as he got closer and snatched the ball from the water's surface. "Oh my, this is so dang cold!" And quickly he leapt out of the water. "Ow, ow, and the rocks!"

"Oh come on..." Bizzy laughed. "It's not that bad."

Luigi stood at the edge, and when Jacko came out of the water, he started to jump for the ball. "Oh no, little guy, oh no."

After a while, Jacko threw the ball up the beach. He went to where his shoes and socks were and sat on the beach. "I can't feel my feet."

Bizzy laughed a good hearty laugh from the gut.

Jacko looked down and something red caught his eye. "Look, a piece of red sea glass!"

Luigi ran back faster than before. He dropped the ball right at Jacko's feet. And then the ball started to roll back toward the water.

Jacko ran for it. Luigi stood there and looked up at Bizzy.

"Not funny, Luigi, not funny." Something about the dog's face told Bizzy that he was laughing.

The End

ALSO BY TJ COSTELLO

Next Book in this Series

Secret of the Broken Sea Glass

Want to Know How Luigi came to adopt Bizzy?

Download the prequel, *Puppy Love and Peril*, for free at

tjcostellowriter.com/newsletter

ABOUT THE AUTHOR

TJ Costello is a writer, photographer and teacher in New England. When she's not plotting murders (in her cozy mysteries), she's walking her dog, St. Peter "Petey," reading mysteries, taking photographs, and watching movies. Sometimes she just sits and watches the sea because she's blessed to live in a coastal town in New England.

She loves to hear from readers so contact her at tj@tjcostellowriter.com.

Sign-up for her newsletter by visiting her website tjcostellowriter.com/newsletter for news, giveaways, and most especially for *Petey's Thoughts*, where Petey tells you what it's like to live with a cozy mystery writer.